Wild THING

NEW YORK TIMES BESTSELLING AUTHOR

JA HUSS

Edited by RJ Locksley
Cover Design by JA Huss
Cover photo: Sara Eirew

Kidnapping her was the easy part.
Now I've got to tame her.
Runaway corporate princess, Lyssa Baylor, was born
with a silver spoon in her mouth.
But that's not what I'll be sticking in there.

LYSSA

Freelance princess hunter, Mason Macintyre, thinks
he's so tough with those bulging muscles. He thinks
he's so smart with his plan to tame me with spankings
and submission.

Well, I've got news for him. They don't call me Wild
Thing for nothing. I've been playing unruly princess
my whole life and I'm not about to stop now.

MASON

This was supposed to be a simple kidnap job. Catch
her and bring her in so she can be married off to the
son of a family friend.

But once her father realizes the man he hired to reform
his unruly brat of a daughter won't be able to handle
her, he blackmails me into completing the job.

No one blackmails me, I don't care how rich and powerful you are. Her father might be untouchable, but Lyssa isn't.

I'm gonna touch her all over and punish her so hard, that forced marriage will be her only way out of my little princess reform school.

WILD THING is a smokin'-hot, sexy story of a runaway princess and her reluctant Prince Charming. A tantalizing tale of forced marriage, captive submission, and a hero who doesn't know he's a hero until he meets the girl he was meant to save.

CHAPTER ONE

The club is the kind of place I'd have liked back before I knew better. Red velvet rope caging in a long line in front, trendy-ish people standing in it, tough guy at the door trying to keep those people out.

I never understood this. I mean, I get the bouncers. I've bounced many a club in my day. But why do people stand in line? Hopeful. Waiting. Wasting their Saturday night.

Don't they get it? They're not good enough. That line isn't there because the club is crowded inside, it's there to keep them out.

I want to walk up to every single person standing in this line and shake the fuck out of them. Tell them to get a life, or at the very least, go do something else besides beg this asshole at the door to let them play with the cool kids.

That's not what happens.

Instead I shove my hands into the pockets of my jeans, meet the eyes of the bouncer at the door as he unhooks the velvet rope, and slide on past him without comment.

It's a work night. I don't have time to babysit the masses.

Inside it's predictable. Too fucking loud. Too fucking dark. Too fucking hot.

And this club is crowded. So maybe I was wrong about those assholes in line outside. In fact, it's probably over capacity, so yeah. OK. I was wrong about that.

But none of my other opinions about this club, or the people inside it, will change tonight. That's for sure.

I sigh, glancing around at the hundreds of men, all dressed smart casual and looking like good little drones. So alike, I can't even begin to understand what women see when they scan the crowd like predators, trying to choose one to take home tonight.

Most of the men are in light colors because the beach is just a block over and that's pretty much the dress code around here. Tight, white t-shirts with a short, perfectly tailored tan linen jacket, rounded out with chinos and boring loafers on their feet.

Not me. I'm all in navy blue. Tonight I'm sporting my version of smart casual. I have on a button-down shirt, expensive, well-worn jeans with a black belt, a short cotton jacket pressed to perfection, and black, polished dress boots.

Every man in here was chosen at the door to be a part of the scenery because that's the meat-market expectation. But even though I also meet that expectation, that's not why that bouncer let me in. I greased his palm earlier in the day with five crisp Benjamins.

Still, I reluctantly admit that I fit in. All the ladies look my way as I push my way through the crowd, scanning faces for my target. Some of them wink. One even grabs my ass.

I don't even turn around to see who that was.

I studied up on the dress code for tonight because I don't want to be in this place any longer than I have to. This is not where I shop for meat and none of these half-dressed girls are worth my time. Not even the one I came for.

Though that's not completely true or I wouldn't be here, would I? I need her for something. It's just not sex.

And I'm not being a dick about this. Not really. I know their type. Rich girls. Privileged girls. Bratty girls. The kind with snarky comments on the tips of their tongues and condescending looks in their eyes. The kind who think the world owes them a good time every second of the day. The kind who run away from their fiancés because they don't *love* them.

Like it matters. They're gonna play house for a few years, maybe have a kid or two, and then they'll get divorced and go back on the market to do it all again.

Maybe I'm a cynic? I dunno. The whole thing is so fucking pointless.

But what do I care? "It's a job," I whisper under my breath. Find her, take her out back, throw her in the back of the van. Drive her back to her father. Collect my money.

Simple. I'll be out of here in ten minutes tops.

I glance up at the VIP area and spot her immediately.

She's hard to miss.

Skin-tight gold dresses kinda have that effect under the strobe lights.

Seriously, it's gold. And it hugs her curves like a second skin. Revealing her large breasts—probably fake, they are that spectacular—and accentuating her tiny waist. The back is open all the way down to her ass. Two thin straps hold up the low-cut front and meld into the fabric that runs down her sides. Curving in towards her stomach and revealing her hip bones.

I just want to shake my head at that dress. Sexy as fuck, for sure. But no way in *hell* would I let any woman I know walk out in public wearing it. Especially to a club.

She shimmers under the flashing strobe lights like the sun flashing across a summer pond. Her long, blonde hair flips back and forth with her head as she dances. Not really with someone, but surrounded by men in tan linen jackets, tight, white t-shirts, and loafers on their feet.

Like I said. Predictable.

She is Lyssa Baylor.

She is so rich, her little dog has a trust fund.

She is so privileged, her daddy didn't give her a car for her sixteenth birthday, he gave her a yacht.

She is so popular, she didn't even enter by the front door.

And she is so well taken care of there's a limo driving around the block, ready to pick her up in the back alley the moment she decides to leave.

I think I hate her immediately.

But she sees me coming. Her eyes find mine, then flit away as if she's not interested.

She is though. That's why I'm wearing this stupid smart-casual outfit. I know how to catch the eye of any woman on the planet. And I'm not bragging, it's just true. Her family has more money than they can spend in a hundred lifetimes and I… well, I just have these looks.

Six foot two, hundred and ninety-seven pounds of muscle, brown hair light enough to go blonde in the summer, and green eyes that force you to look at my face—then notice my perfectly square jaw with just the right amount of stubble.

The double-take gets its name from how women react the first time they see *me*.

I don't stop at the red velvet rope leading up to the VIP area. I greased that bouncer's palm earlier today too. So I slide easily into Lyssa's world without fuss, or comment, or care.

"Drink?" a waitress asks immediately. She smiles at me, eyes locked on mine.

Told you. My emerald peepers get that job *done*.

"No, thanks," I say, charming her even further with my smile. "I'm not staying."

"No?" she says, batting her eyes at me. "That's a shame."

I place a hand on her shoulder and squeeze it a little, aware that this is against personal-space protocol, but not caring, either. "Maybe I'll see you around next weekend," I say, winking at her before I move on through the crowd.

"Sure," she calls back. "I'm here every Saturday!"

"I'm sure you are," I mumble, already making my way over towards Lyssa.

I pass by a waitress carrying a tray of champagne flutes, grab one, then wink at her too and place a twenty on the tray. "Thanks," I say.

She giggles and says, "No problem," as she continues on like nothing happened.

The little fast-acting pill is already in my fingertips and a moment later I've dropped it in the glass. It bubbles at the bottom, but I tested this out earlier today. And this particular gem will be thoroughly dissolved by the time I push my way through the crowd and reach Lyssa.

She scans the crowd, looking for her next target the same way I was scanning for mine when I walked in this club.

When she sees me, she stops looking and smiles. I smile back, then look away. Because that's how you play this game.

Just because I hate this scene doesn't mean I don't know the rules.

When I look back at Lyssa a few moments later, some guy just off to her left is leaning in to her ear, whispering something. Her face goes serious, then she smiles and nods her head at him, flashing her bright, white teeth.

Little quickie in the bathroom, Lyssa? I imagine him asking her.

Sure, be right there, she answers.

Not really. But it's probably close enough.

She leaves the dance floor, walks over to a booth, grabs her purse, and pulls out a wad of cash.

Oh, what do we have here? Little deal going down?

You disappoint me, Lyssa. That was not casual or even remotely sneaky.

Wild Thing, they call her. Her father, her fiancé, hell, even her friends call her that.

And she sure does look the part. Dark eyeshadow smokes up her blue eyes and her hair is a mess of unruly long, blonde waves. The kind of hair that perpetually looks like she just got done fucking someone. And her skin is glistening with just the right amount of sweat to make you think of sex on a hot summer night.

She hands the money to the guy, who has followed her over to the table, and smiles at him, nodding her head towards the bathrooms. I read her lips as she says, "Twenty minutes, OK?"

He nods. I can't see what he says because his back is to me. But I don't need to. I know his answer.

She, like me, gets whatever she wants when it comes to sex.

That's how I'm gonna trap her tonight.

That's how I'm gonna get her good and drugged and in my van.

In five minutes she's gonna want sex with me.

And even though she's not gonna get it—that's not in my contract—I'm ready to make her think she will.

CHAPTER TWO

This week started out bad and only got worse.

My father is back. Not that I ever thought he'd completely disappear, but I had hopes. It's been two years since he really bothered me. There was one iffy moment last summer when he tried to tell me what to do and how to act. And that one weirdo who attacked me in an alley a couple months ago and made me morph into fight mode. But I'm not positive that last one was my father. I tell myself it wasn't because I need to believe. Can't be sure though.

I think I shut my father down well enough this week to make him disappear back into the shadows he oozed out of for a while.

I think.

I hope.

I need to believe.

My father was tenacious, I'll give him that. He called and left messages on Monday and Tuesday, then tried to approach me outside a bookstore on Wednesday, and actually waited for me in my building lobby on Thursday.

I successfully navigated my way through all of that. Then Friday… nothing. I thought maybe he'd gotten the hint.

But no. He called today and left a message that I have duties and I will be fulfilling said duties no matter what.

It left me feeling shaky and scared. My heart palpitating with thoughts of past bad days. Things like getting fingerprinted in police stations, and mug shots, and sentencing.

So what should a girl do when faced with that kind of week?

Party, of course.

So even though I've had a bad week the club is super fun tonight. All my friends from college are here and it's nice to forget about the shit going on in my life, even if it is only for a few hours.

I'm gonna stay until they kick me out. I'm gonna drink, and dance, and maybe, if I'm really lucky, I'll find someone cool to spend the night with.

Can't go home, that's for sure. My father will probably be waiting for me in the lobby again. Or hell, inside my apartment. It used to be a complete sanctuary, but not anymore.

I'm not going to think about that. Not now. All that crap will be waiting for me tomorrow. Right now all I want is a good time.

So we dance. Me and my friends. They are not close friends, but still. Familiar faces are enough right now. I need old habits. I need casual acquaintances. I need something… anything… to take my mind off all the problems swirling around in my brain.

But it would be really nice to meet someone new too.

A stranger. Someone who knows nothing about me and who I am. What I have or what I could do for them. Not that I have much that's my own. It's almost all his, isn't it? That's why most men like me. For him. My powerful step-father.

So when I see the tall guy walking towards me on the other side of the dance floor, my heartbeat picks up speed. He's a possibility. Kinda dark. Dressed in blue, not tan, like every other guy in here. Tight-fitting shirt and jacket, stubble on his face—just the right amount, because I don't do beards—and a look in his eyes that makes me want to stare at him.

I smile. Turn my head a little. Flirting.

He smiles back, then looks quickly away.

Oh, what do we have here? A player? Maybe?

I'm up for a game of Who Can Fake Indifference While Showing Interest. I practically invented that game.

"Lyssa!" someone shouts in my ear.

I turn to see Greg, and almost forget about my bad week. Because this is why I live these days. Greg and all his secrets keep me going. I don't even have to force the smile I flash at him. "Hey!" I say, leaning in to his neck so he can hear me over the thumping music. "What are you doing here?"

"I need the money," he says. "I'm sorry to bother you like this but—"

"No," I say. "No, no, no. It's fine. I have it."

I turn away and push my way through the crowd to the booth where I've stashed my purse under my summer jacket, then take out the cash and turn back to Greg, handing it to him.

"They'd like to talk to you," he says. Looking down at me with his dark eyes.

"Oh," I say. "Is that really necessary?"

I know it's my responsibility to take care of this business, but can't I just have one night where I don't have to deal with problems? I rally, because it's important to look the part, and say, "Twenty minutes, OK?" Because that stranger in blue is still taking up a major part of my slightly drunk mind and I don't want to let him go yet.

"No problem. They're out front. Can't get past the bouncer," he says. "I'll wait out there with them." Then he turns away and pushes his way back through the crowd.

I sigh, then frown, because I don't really want to deal with this right now. I just want to dance, and drink, and forget. And what's waiting for me outside is a reminder.

My past. Hell, my present too.

But when I turn, the handsome one with the flashing eyes is right behind me holding a glass of champagne.

"Drink?" he asks. "I just stole it from a waitress so I could make a good impression. So please," he begs, charming me with a smile that reveals no teeth. One of those sly smiles. Very sexy smiles. And Jesus, when I look him up and down from close proximity, he is the whole package too. "Don't shoot me down," he says. "I don't think my ego could take it tonight."

I make a noise. One of those half grunts, half laughs. Because I'm pretty sure his ego could take it. I'm also pretty sure that no one shoots this man down.

"Mason," he says, leaning down in my ear so he doesn't have to yell over the music.

And then he takes my hand and kisses it.

"Lyssa," I say, momentarily caught up in his spell. I take the drink.

"Nice to meet you, Lyssa."

I think I blush. I never blush. I'm the one who makes men blush. Still, there it is. Heat creeping up my neck that makes all the hairs stand on end. "You too, Mason. I've never seen you here before. New in town?"

"Sure," he says. Like he's agreeing with me, but that's not really true.

"Come to Billionaire Beach often?"

"No," he says. "You?"

"All the time," I say. "We have a house here." Not that I'm staying there. But it's not a lie. We do have a house here. All my friends from college do. And if this handsome devil didn't just appear, I'd crash with one of them when the fun was over. But hey… there's no law that says I have to go home with someone from Billionaire Beach now, is there?

He does one of those nods. The chin-lift kind. A nod of understanding, not really agreement.

Good going, Lyssa. One sentence and he's already pegged you for what you really are. A spoiled little socialite.

"You wanna go somewhere and talk?" he asks.

I look at my watch. Because I did tell Greg twenty minutes.

"Or have you already made plans with that guy who just left?"

I huff a laugh. "Someone's been paying attention."

"I tend to do that when I see something I like."

"You like me, do you?" I take a sip of the champagne, trying to appear nonchalant. Then take another because he's just… staring at me. Almost hungrily. A shudder of desire shoots through my body.

"I like what I see so far," he says, smiling again. Then he laughs. "That's lame, right? I'm so off my game tonight. Don't judge me, OK? I've had a bad week."

"Oh." I laugh. "No, I won't if you won't." I laugh again. Only this time it's a giggle.

I take another drink, then decide to just down it all in one gulp. I'm acting like a fool. Like a stupid schoolgirl.

And he doesn't look like a man who dates schoolgirls. He's definitely older than most people in this club. Over thirty for sure.

But I like it. I like it a lot. Older man. Younger woman. That's hot.

"So who'd you come here with?" I ask.

"Just me," he says, panning his hand down his body.

Which makes me take a second look. And then a third. Damn. He is very sexy.

"So what do you say?" he asks.

"Hmmm?" I mumble, unable to stop staring at his brilliant green eyes.

"Talk?" He laughs. "You wanna go somewhere and talk? This really isn't my scene. I just came out tonight because I didn't want to be alone."

Oh, God. I'm dead. Because there is no way I'm not going home with him. It's a humanitarian crisis. "You're lonely?" I ask in disbelief.

"Don't believe me?"

"Not for a second." I giggle. I really need another drink. Or maybe I've drunk too much? I suddenly feel pretty buzzed.

"Come on," he says, taking my hand and pulling me through the crowd. "I know a quiet place."

And before I can even think twice, I'm following him. I dump my empty champagne flute on a table as we pass by, and then he's leading me down the stairs of the VIP section, and towards the back of the club to the secret door where only me, and a few other important guests, get to enter and exit.

So… he's somebody important, that's for sure.

By the time we get through the crowd down on the main dance floor and walk through the maze of hallways that lead to the back exit, I'm stumbling.

He stops at the door and looks at me with concern. "You OK, Lyssa?"

I push my wild hair away from my eyes and nod. "Sure. I'm good."

But when he opens the door and tugs me through it out into the dark, empty alley, I'm not sure I am.

Something is wrong with me.

The cool night air hits my face and I draw in a deep breath of relief.

Maybe it was just too hot in there. Because the wind refreshes me for a moment.

He stops in the alley and turns around, smiling.

"Better?" he says, his voice low now. Kinda growly and sexy.

"Hmmm, yeah," I say, pushing my hair up off my forehead to let the air flow over me. "Much better."

"You buzzed?" he asks. "I can get you a ride home if you're not up to talking."

He pulls out his phone, like he's about to summon an Uber. But I place a hand over his phone and say, "No, no. I'm good."

He smiles again. God, that smile should be illegal.

"Then come on. There's a little alcove over here where we can have some privacy."

I follow him. Mostly because he's still got a hold of my hand and he's tugging me along. But also because… I really don't feel right.

I'm stumbling, and dizzy, and a little bit nauseated.

"Take off your shoes," he says, stopping and bending down. He reaches for my ankle and his touch… Oh, God. His touch is soft and sends chills up my back. I actually forget about how sick I feel and picture him fucking me.

He slips off one gold shoe, sets it on the cement, then reaches for the other ankle and takes that shoe off too.

"Don't worry," he says, picking up my shoes in one hand and placing his other hand on my elbow to lead me. "I'll take care of them for you. This way you won't trip and fall. I can't bring you in damaged."

I laugh at that, finding it unreasonably funny.

Until the meaning of his words actually hits my brain and I realize what he just said.

"What?" I say groggily.

He looks over his shoulder as he pulls me around a corner and smiles.

And that's when I see the van.

That's when I realize what's really happening here.

He charmed me.

Drugged me.

And now he's gonna take me.

CHAPTER THREE

She stops dead in the alley as fear floods past the drug I slipped into her champagne.

Some guys might panic at this. Some guys might worry she'll scream and that the people on the beach, less than a hundred yards away, will hear her. Some guys… but not this guy.

This is what I do.

Her father hired me because I'm the best. And believe me, I've dealt with every kind of capture scenario there is. And all of them were big men, like me. All of them could put up a real fight. And none of them were stupid enough to accept a drink from a stranger in a fucking nightclub.

So I don't panic and I don't worry.

I just smile. "What's wrong?" I ask. "You OK, princess?"

She makes a face at me. If she wasn't drugged I might worry. Because I've heard how she reacted to the last guy who attempted to bring her in a few months ago.

"Where are we going?" she asks, swaying a little.

"Just right here," I say, slipping my hands around her waist and backing up into a wall. Then I lean down into her neck and kiss her, whispering, "We wanted some privacy, right?"

She hesitates. Like maybe this isn't what she thought.

It is, but she wants to believe me. They all want to believe they're gonna get one more chance. One more day of freedom. That I'm not the one who brings them in.

I just need to string her along for a few minutes and let the drug overtake her. Then I throw her in the van, drive her up to some private country estate, and collect my payment.

So fucking easy.

"You don't want to kiss me, Lyssa?" I ask. "Because I'm only here for one night. So… last chance."

She tilts her head up. Eyes locked on mine. Smiles.

And then she knees me in the balls.

I am wearing a cup. I come prepared for all possible scenarios. But that shit still hurts enough for me to double over.

It's one second. Just one.

But they don't call her Wild Thing for nothing.

She turns and runs.

Bolts down the alley and I chase her. She's mostly stumbling forward on momentum alone, but she's still fast.

I dig down and stretch my long legs out, pumping my arms to gain speed. Then, just before she reaches the corner, I snatch her by the back of her dress. She crashes backwards into my chest, knocking me off balance a little.

She turns on me, teeth bared, eyes wild, and drags her perfectly manicured fingernails down the side of my cheek.

Oh. No, she didn't.

We both stop, momentarily stunned.

And then she's running again. This time in the other direction, right towards the van.

I go after her. It's a long back alley. So even though people are so close we can hear them laughing and partying on the beach, they are on the other side of all these buildings.

I stretch my arm again, but this time the second I get a hold of the strap on her dress, she whirls around with fists raised.

This snaps the strap on her dress, and it falls down, revealing one of her large, round, naked breasts.

I'm more concerned about that than she is, because she doesn't pause or even let out a gasp of rage.

She just punches me in the face.

And damn, that little fist packs some power. My jaw slides to the right a little and I stop to look at her.

She punches me again.

But I grab her by both wrists and pull her in to my body, then quickly turn her around. One arm around her waist, one hand cupped over her mouth so she can't scream.

"You're gonna pay for that," I growl into her neck. Then urge her forward with my hips, kneeing her legs at the same time, letting her know we are walking now.

She's screaming beneath my hand. Trying to bite me. And her body is wriggling and squirming. Her ass is pressing against my groin, and even though I'm wearing a cup, I can feel that.

I can feel all of that and my cock begins to flood with blood, finding this whole thing more than a little erotic.

"Stop it," I hiss, more pissed at myself right now than I am about her struggle. Because this little fight with her is turning me on.

There is no doubt Lyssa Baylor is beautiful. She's one of those golden girls, but at the same time, there's a bleak tragic look to her. I like that look. Lost, dark, desperate, wild girls are kinda my thing.

Just… not *this* wild girl.

She continues to wriggle and my cock continues to grow. There's also the added fact that her bare nipple rubs against my arm around her waist each time she bends forward, trying to shake me loose.

"Stop it," I say again. "I'm not gonna hurt you."

She screams in my hand, shaking her head back and forth like a wild animal.

I drag her towards the van. It's very close. She really helped me out in that department. But she resists and fights every step of the way. Still kicking and screaming. Still trying to bite me and still rocking her body backwards and forwards until her fucking naked tit is cupped underneath my arm.

God. It's so soft and squishy. *Surprise, surprise, Mason. You were wrong—they are most definitely real.*

That kinda turns me on too.

Get your head together. You're in the middle of a capture job. Throw her ass in the van and get the hell out of here.

Right. Do not think about how one more tug on that dress will rip it right off her.

I finally manage to get her to the back of the van, amazed that no one has happened upon our little struggle, but then realize that whole thing probably took less than a minute.

It's cool, I tell myself. *It's all good.*

I unwrap my arm from around her waist, holding her tightly with the hand I still have over her mouth. She's breathing hard into it. And her hair is covering her face and mine too as I reach for the handle on the van.

She writhes, breaking free. She's already running when I take off after her and reach out, grab at her dress and then…

Yup.

I do it.

I rip it right off her.

She slows. Just enough for me to wrap both my arms around her, swing her around, stumble forward, and throw her into the back of the van.

She falls into it on all fours with a hard thump, her bare ass up in the air.

I reach in without thinking and slap her cheek hard. Hard enough to make her squeal and turn around, baring her pussy and her breasts in the same instant.

"My dress!" she says, weak and groggy.

Fucking drug is finally overpowering her.

I look at the dress on the ground, just a useless scrap of fabric now, and shrug. Throw it in as evidence. Because her father is gonna be pissed if she shows up naked.

"That's what you get," I say, breathing hard from our fight. "You little brat."

I start to close up the door and she squeaks out, "My Choos!"

"What?" I ask though the crack in the door, thinking she's just wasted now.

"My Jimmy Choos! My shoes!"

She's naked, legs spread open to reveal her bare pussy, and her perfect tits are bouncing as she scrambles to sit up.

And she's worried about her *shoes?*

I slam the door shut and I'm just about to walk around and get in the driver's side when I spot the shoes on the ground where I dropped them after she ran.

"Fuck," I say, walking over to scoop them up. I get in the van, open the little window to the back, and throw them through. "There's your fucking shoes."

Wild thing.

I sigh. Blood running down my face from her scratches. My jaw aching from her punches. My balls definitely unhappy, even with the protection of the cup.

And my cock is hard.

Because I'm a man and I can't help it.

That shit was *hot*.

CHAPTER FOUR

I sit there in the dark after he slams the door closed. A few seconds later a window opens above my head, and he says, "There's your fucking shoes," as he tosses them through. One of them hits me in the head and the other drops into my lap.

I really didn't need that. My head is already pounding and my vision is blurry. I reach down into my lap to push the shoe away and realize I'm naked.

I knew that.

I just forgot.

How? How did I forget that?

Oh, yeah. This charming bastard drugged my drink.

What a total fuckup I am. I know better than to drink anything at a club that I didn't buy myself and didn't have eyes on the whole time. I know better.

But he charmed me. Those eyes, and that smile. And his body.

What the fuck is wrong with me? Am I daydreaming about the man who just abducted me?

I try to turn around, intent on banging on the window. Demanding that I be let out. But I'm too tired. Too wasted.

My body slumps instead of sitting up and that's when I realize I'm on a mattress and there's a blanket. It takes me whole minutes to rearrange my body so I'm not only underneath the blanket, but lying down in a position that doesn't make me feel like I was just dumped in a van.

For some reason my ass is stinging.

The motion of the drive is sorta soothing and I find myself nodding off. Too sleepy and groggy to keep my eyes open or even try to come up with an escape plan.

Besides, he said he wasn't gonna hurt me.

Oh, Lyssa, that still-sober part of my brain says. *You're delusional.*

No one abducts a pretty, young girl with no intention of hurting them.

"Yeah," I hear him say on the other side of the window.

Mason. His name is Mason. I remember that much.

"I got her. I'm on my way now."

Who is he talking to? Where are we going?

"A little bit," he says. "Not much."

Pause.

"You know. Typical girl fight."

Girl fight? Did he just insult me? I think I did pretty good considering he's like eight inches taller than me, seventy pounds heavier, and he *drugged* me.

I kicked fucking ass, is what I did. That was not a fair fight.

"She's fine. We should be there in about three hours."

Pause.

Three hours. I force my brain to think about what's three hours away from Billionaire Beach and then I gasp. "Oh, no," I moan.

"What?" he says. And for a second I think he's talking to me. "That wasn't the deal." Then I realize he's not. He's talking to whoever's on the phone. "Mr. Baylor—"

"What?" I gasp.

"—I told you my terms. I'll be there in three hours and you had better be waiting. I'm a bounty hunter, not a goddamned babysitter."

I make myself get up on my knees. And that's not easy. I'm very drugged, but it's not getting worse. It's not getting better, it's just not getting worse. So either he gave me something that isn't supposed to completely knock me out, or he gave me a very low dose of something that is.

I pound on the window. "No!" I yell. "No! Let me out!"

"Yes," he says. "That's her."

Pause.

"I didn't give her much. Just enough to throw her in the van."

Pause.

"Dude," he says, clearly irritated with my stepfather. Because that's who's on the other end of this phone conversation. That's who hired him to abduct me. "I'm a fucking professional. I think I know what I'm doing." He hangs up after that. Mumbles, "Fucking asshole."

Yes. My stepfather is a fucking asshole. Because this isn't about me. This is about him. He's forcing me to marry his business partner's son. Dickerson Worthington the Third. Can you believe there are three fucking Dickersons running around this country?

I refuse to marry a man named Dickerson. I don't care if my stepfather's partnership depends on it. How does that even make sense, anyway? How could me marrying Dickerson the Third fix his business? It makes no sense. And who names a baby boy Dickerson anyway? It's like his parents said, "I think we'd like our son to grow up to be a dick."

Because Dickerson is a dick. And he's got a small one too. He pulled it out on me once in summer camp and… Oh, God, I want to vomit just thinking about his shriveled-up little pecker.

I pound on the window again. "Please!" I beg. "You don't understand what you're doing."

"Shut up," he growls. "Or I'll spank that ass of yours again."

Oh. That's why it stings. I remember now. He slapped me and I was so stunned I just kinda looked at him with my mouth open.

But I wasn't stunned that it hurt. Though it did. He smacked me hard.

I was stunned because it kinda got me hot for a second. I don't know why I like the thought of shit like that. The spanking, I mean. I just do. Especially when it's all real… and angry… and sexy.

You're so stupid, Lyssa. Certifiably sick.

"You don't understand," I say again. But it's a weak, small mumble and I don't even think he hears me.

I slump back down onto the mattress and cover back up, my eyelids too heavy to cooperate with my big plans of talking my way out of this little kidnap adventure. I fall asleep to the rocking motion of the van. Aware that my life is over. My freedom is being taken away. And in two weeks I will have to marry Dickerson. I will have to let him kiss me, and dance with me, all in front of people.

And I'll have to smile through the whole miserable experience.

Then the real humiliation starts. Because I will be locked in a bedroom with him and forced to consummate the vows.

So. Gross.

No, this can't be happening. I won't do it.

I say that over, and over, and *over* again in my head. As if summoning courage and determination is enough to put a stop sign out in front of my billionaire stepfather's best-laid plans and turn this shit show around.

But it's not enough. It's never been enough. He has done worse than this to me, but I've been free. For two whole years, I've managed to slip away. I had the apartment and… the money. Though I knew what that money was.

His bribe.

I didn't spend it, of course. Not on *me*. But he doesn't know that and now he's coming to collect what he paid for.

I foolishly thought this freedom would last forever. I let down my guard and allowed myself to believe my life was my own and now…

 But… I won't do it. I won't. I will find a way out of this arrangement he's made for me if it's the last thing I do. I will not marry that pervert. I will not give him my body. They'll have to hold me down and tie me to the bed before I submit to that.

When I wake up I realize it's because the van has stopped.

I have a raging headache and my eyes feel like someone rubbed sandpaper over them while I slept. And my body aches. My arms are stiff, my back has a kink in it, and I'm cold.

The driver's door opens, then slams shut. Shoes crunch on a gravel driveway and my worst fear comes true.

I know where we're at.

The mansion my stepfather bought me when I turned eighteen. The very mansion where the wedding will be held in two weeks. I should've known this. I should've seen this coming. I knew my stepfather was dead serious about forcing this marriage. He told me. Yelled it at me the last time I found him waiting in the lobby of my building. He dragged me into the elevator and yelled, so loud and angry, the veins were sticking out of his neck. I stood and let him. Just let him berate me, all the while wishing he'd have a stroke.

Which is horrible, but he's horrible. No decent stepfather would make their only daughter marry a man like Dickerson. He's… they're *both*… awful, awful people.

And he threatened me that day. Threatened to 'beat the brat right out of me,' as he put it. Complained about how I used him for money, and all I cared about was clubbing, and drinking, and friends. He's never had a single nice thing to say to me. Ever. Not since my mother married him when I was six.

Not even the day she died. He told me I looked like a drugged-up slut at the funeral.

I didn't used to care that he hated me. Why should I? I was the light of my mother's life and she let me know that every moment I was home from boarding school. And yes, I did get everything I wanted, but I was not a bad girl. I didn't hurt people. Not with words, not with actions, not with violence. I got straight A's, I excelled in all the school clubs, I even ran charity events with my mother every summer when I was home.

And OK, yeah. I mostly did that so I didn't have to see my stepfather or be subjected to his house rules while I was on break, but it was nice to spend that time with my mom and I don't regret it.

I was the perfectly poised little rich girl any time we were in public and people could see me.

And I used to have real friends. Before my stepfather ripped me out of my boarding school when I was fifteen and made me come home and go to school with the sons and daughters of all his horrible friends.

Like Dickerson. Gross.

Then… everything changed. Me, mostly. But it wasn't my fault.

And then my mother passed away two years ago and suddenly I was no one's light. I was just… Wild Thing.

That's what he called me.

Wild thing.

Like I'm an animal.

Fuck him.

When he ambushed me on Thursday I got lucky. He couldn't drag me out of the lobby, not without me making a scene. So he grabbed my arm tight and told me to get in the elevator and once we got upstairs we would wait until his people came to take me away in the middle of the night.

So I could "get the help I needed".

He said I was ruining his reputation, and his business, and his life.

What about *my* life? He's the one who ruined that.

And me too.

He *ruined* me.

No, Lyssa. I chastise myself for falling back into that old belief. I've worked hard on my issues. So I drink a little too much? And I party hard. And go dancing. He made me this girl, didn't he?

Yes, my inner voice soothes.

It's all his fault I'm wild.

But when we got off the elevator on my floor there were housekeepers in the hallway. And I knew… if I did not make a scene—the biggest scene I've ever made in my entire life—if I did not become the personification of *Wild Thing,* then everything would go back to the way it was.

And I would not allow that to happen.

My freedom was too important.

So I did. And I won that day.

But I'm not going to win this one.

The back door to the van opens and Mason the Princess Hunter stands there, backlit by the lights at the front of the mansion.

"Get out," he says.

I'm still under the covers. My body hidden from him. But if I get out it won't be.

"I don't have clothes," I mumble, my throat so dry, my voice cracks.

"Whose fault is that?" he asks.

"You ripped my dress off, you fucking asshole."

He smiles. It's the same smile as last night, but how I ever thought it was charming, I'll never know. Because I see it for what it is now. Evil. He is evil. "You ran," he says.

"Yeah, because you fucking drugged my drink and were about to stuff me into this van." I hiss out that whole sentence.

"You know what?" he says, pointing his finger at me. "I don't like your filthy fucking mouth."

I practically guffaw. "You don't like my filthy fucking mouth?"

"No," he says. "I think it's disgusting. And if you were my daughter I'd slap your ass every time those words flew out."

"Ever hear of leading by example?" I snarl.

"Get out."

"I don't have clothes. I'm not gonna give you the pleasure of seeing me naked again."

He smiles, and once again, it's evil. "You wanna play that game, princess? Because I'll play."

And then he reaches under my covers, grabs my ankle, and pulls me out of the van.

She slides to the edge of the van. I grab her shoulders, spin her around so she's face down, and push down between her shoulder blades so her perfect ass is up in the air.

And then I swat her.

Hard.

She bucks her back and squeals. "You motherfucker!"

I slap her again. So hard, my hand is stinging.

"You wanna be a little wild thing?" I ask her. "I'll show you what that gets you when I'm in charge." I smack her one more time. And this makes her whimper. "Had enough?" I ask, breathing heavy. "Because I can go all day."

"You're a dick!"

One last time. I make it count.

"Ow!" she screams. "You—"

"Stop fighting, Lyssa. For once in your life, just do as you're told. Because you can't win. You can scream all you want, there's nothing around here for miles. You can't even run because you don't have clothes."

She starts breathing funny. Like maybe she's crying. So I figure that last one did the trick. I grab her arm and pull her up, then spin her around.

For a second she almost tries to cover herself. But instead, she tilts up her chin, squares her shoulders, and looks me in the eyes. Daring me to find her sexy.

Which I do. There's no way to deny that. But her attitude. Oh, fuck that. I do not put up with girls like Lyssa.

She has tears in her eyes, but she's not crying. Those are tears of anger.

I know the difference.

"Gonna behave now?" I ask.

She tips her chin up even higher. Looking down her nose at me. She's got that haughty princess act down, that's for sure. No one's gonna knock her down a peg. Especially a guy like me.

That look says I'm not worthy of her anger. I'm not even worthy of her contempt.

And honestly, I don't really give a fuck. She's not my problem anymore. All I gotta do is take her inside, lock her up, and wait for her stepfather to show up with some asshole he hired to give his stepdaughter the attitude adjustment she so very badly needs.

"Good," I say, taking her silence as submission. "Come with me."

I hold her arm tight. Probably too tight. But she did try to run. Twice. So I'm not taking any chances. It's four in the morning, I've been driving for hours, and I'm not in the mood to go chasing her across that wide-open lawn in the front of the house. She probably wouldn't make it to the woods, but you never know with this girl.

Just thinking about hunting her down in those dark woods pisses me off and it hasn't even happened.

Not gonna, either. Because I grip her so hard, she whimpers.

"You're going to bruise me," she protests as I drag her up the impressive front stairs to the mansion.

"You mean like you bruised my jaw?" I ask.

"You kidnapped me! What did you expect?"

I shake her a little and say, "Just be quiet," as I punch in the security code for the house and swing the door open wide.

She resists, but I pull her through the door, then close it, and lock it up tight. "You know this house?" I ask her.

"Yes," she growls.

"Good. Then you know the security system it has. Every window is locked. Every door is locked. If you break a window and try to get out, this system won't call the police, Lyssa. It calls in a whole team of guys like me who will not simply spank your ass and demand respect. They will hunt you down, shoot you with tranquilizers, and then tie you up in your bedroom. So think very carefully before you make yet another bad decision in your life. Because it will get ugly."

I shove her. Hard. Probably harder than I need to. But I want her to understand that I'm not fucking around. I need her to behave for just a few hours so I can collect my payment and get the fuck on my way. Forget I ever met this girl or her miserable stepfather.

I flick on the light and find her standing in the middle of the opulent foyer, her back to me.

And damn, I really did spank her hard. One ass cheek has a bright red handprint on it.

She takes a deep breath.

Lets it out.

But doesn't turn around.

I take a moment to study her backside, that urge inside from earlier resurfacing. Because she is stunningly beautiful, even from this view.

Then I picture her pussy in the van, her legs spread open wide, her bouncing breasts, and begin to get hard again.

I need to take this fucking cup off. I can't believe I drove three hours wearing that stupid thing.

But good thing you had it, Mason. Otherwise this night might've gone a little different. You might not be here right now. And as much as I hate to admit it, I took this job for a reason. A very urgent reason and I need that payment from her stepfather. I have big plans, all of which depend on seeing this through.

She looks over her shoulder at me. Frowning. Almost pouting.

"Not gonna work," I say, shaking my head. "You can pout those plump lips all you want. Not gonna work on me."

She huffs and turns to face me. Unashamed of her naked body. Maybe even quite proud of it. "I'm not pouting at you. In case you didn't notice, I'm having a personal crisis right now. This isn't about *you*."

I toss the keys to the van on a nearby table. She can't get out of the house, so there's no reason to worry about the keys. "In case you didn't already figure it out," I say, "everything I do is about me, Lyssa. So I won't be joining your pity party."

She shrugs one shoulder. "Good. You weren't invited."

"Go put some clothes on."

"I don't live here," she snaps. "This might be my house, but I have no intention of *ever* living here. So there are no clothes. I guess you should have thought of that before you ripped my dress right off my body."

I laugh. "You always go out clubbing wearing no panties and no bra, Lyssa? Is that the image you like to project?"

"That's none of your business," she says.

"You wanted to fuck me in the alley," I say.

"No," she says. "You wanted to fuck *me*."

"Sweetheart," I say, laughing a little. "I can fuck anyone I want. And believe me, you're just another little girl pretending to be a woman. I wouldn't waste my time with you. So you can stand there naked all you want, it's not gonna help your situation. So go. Find. Some clothes."

"I just told you—"

"They're in the goddamned bedroom," I say. "Your stepfather put them there."

She licks her lips and smiles. "Well, maybe you can point me to said bedroom? Because as I've already explained, I don't live here."

Well. She's got game. I'll give her that. Trying to get me up in her bedroom.

"No," she says, even though I didn't say anything. "I'm not trying to get you up in my bedroom. I just really have no idea where it might be."

I look up at the second floor. There are actually two staircases in the foyer. Both of them snake down from either side of the large, wide space.

Wings, I decide. This place has wings. Pretentious much?

But what did I expect? Her stepfather has the kind of money most people can't even comprehend. He owns half of the office buildings in downtown, more properties in the upper north side than I can count and some government official even let this asshole put his name on a park.

"Up there," I say, nodding to the second floor.

She tosses her head, making her wildly disheveled hair cover half of her face. "Do you have any idea how many bedrooms this house has?"

I don't even try to guess. A house this size makes no sense to me.

"Twenty-one," she says, answering her own question.

I laugh out loud. "Why the fuck do you need twenty-one bedrooms? You running an orphanage or something?"

She makes a face. "I didn't buy this house, Mason." She crosses her arms, maybe starting to become aware of her nakedness. Or maybe she's just cold. "My stepfather thought he could use it to bribe me to marry his business partner's son. And when it didn't work, he hired you to bring me here and *force* me to marry him."

"Poor you," I say, thinking she's probably cold. Because I can still see one nipple and it's bunched up and hard.

"Yeah," she says, sadness in her voice. "Poor me."

Then she turns, chooses the staircase on the left, and begins to walk up.

I follow her. Because even though I know the security system is top-notch, there's no telling what she'll do.

Besides, I want to look at that handprint on her ass a little more.

It's pretty fucking nice. And if I thought I could get away with it, I'd snap a picture and jerk off to it later. I'd make sure to snap that pic as she was lifting her leg too. Because each time she does that, I get a little rear-view glimpse of her shaved pussy.

"Nice view, isn't it?" she asks, glancing over her shoulder.

I shrug. "Hey," I say, refusing to be ashamed for being caught in the act. "You're the one who wants to show it off. Don't blame me for looking."

The thing is… I do kinda want to fuck her. I think any man in my present situation would be thinking the same thing. Lyssa Baylor is way out of my league. Not in the one-night stand sense. I could get her to one-night-stand me for sure.

But anything more than that and yeah. She's just one of those girls who ignores anyone who doesn't fit neatly into her little delusional bubble.

She stops at the top and looks both ways down the hallway. "Eenie, meany, miney, moe." Then she goes right, even though 'moe' landed on left.

Figures. Wild thing, right? Rebel to the end. God forbid she do anything by direction.

She saunters down the hallway, swaying her hips— probably for my benefit—then grabs the first door handle and swings it open.

"Nope," she says. "Not that one."

"How do you know? You didn't even go in."

"I know," she says. "But feel free. Check the closet. I'll bet you your jacket there's no clothes in there."

I study her for a second. Trying to decide if I should hand over my jacket or make her play the game. Clearly her nakedness is starting to have an effect. She can play tough girl all she wants but you can only be butt naked in front of a strange man for so long before it starts to bother you.

"All you had to do was ask for the jacket, Lyssa. I'd have given it to you."

She shrugs. "This is more entertaining."

"Well, that's not the word I'd use. But whatever. If I was putting this whole insane plan together, I'd choose the first bedroom. So I've got a pretty good feeling you'll lose the bet."

"OK." She smiles. It might even be a genuine smile. Kinda sweet, actually. "Then go check. I'll wait here."

I walk in, flip on the light. It's a nice bedroom. What you'd typically find in a house like this. Professionally decorated in neutral colors. Large, king-sized bed. En suite bathroom.

I pull the closet doors open, find a walk-in. Empty. Then turn back to Lyssa.

She's leaning against the open door, hand out for my jacket. "Told you."

I take off the jacket and give it to her.

She doesn't put it on.

I laugh. "You're too much, you know that?"

I follow her down the hallway to the next door. She throws it open, and says, "Nope. Not this one either."

I walk in, flip on the light. See another version of the last bedroom. Take a deep breath as I walk over to the closet and open it up.

Empty.

I turn back to her. She says, "I think I should get your shirt for this one."

"Ha," I say. "Good one." Then push past her, go to the next door, throw it open, turn on the light, and wait for her decision.

"Nope."

"How do you know that?"

She frowns. Then shrugs. Her tits bouncing a little as she does that. "I just do, that's all."

"So which one is yours? I'm not in the mood to open all twenty-one bedrooms. Don't you want to put something on and just… go to sleep?"

"I sleep naked," she says. "Always have. So it doesn't matter to me."

"Jesus," I say, running my fingers through my hair. "You tire me out, you know that?"

She says nothing.

"You know which room it is, don't you?"

"I have an idea."

"So go there."

She looks down the hallway. Studies it for a moment. Then looks down the other one. The only difference between these two hallways, from what I can tell, is that there's a large double door at the end of the one we're not standing in. And this one has no double door at the end.

If I had to guess, I'd peg that as the master.

God, she's really distracting. Because I could've avoided all this bedroom hide-and-seek if I had just been more aware of my surroundings.

She heads that direction, stops in front of the double doors, and turns back to me. "It's not what you think."

"What?" I say, squinting at her. "What are you talking about?"

She grabs the handles of both doors, swings them open, and she's right.

It's not what I think. Because it's a staircase.

"Where's this go?" I ask.

"To the tower," she says. "Where else does an evil stepfather keep his little corporate princess?"

"What the fuck?" I say, kinda laughing as I step through to go up and look.

But she puts a hand out and says, "I don't think so, Mason. I'm going up alone. Thank you for the escort. I wish I could say it was a pleasure meeting you, but I'm afraid it wasn't." She looks over her shoulder at the staircase, Sighs. Then turns back. "But I'm sure you'll be paid handsomely for your troubles."

And then she throws my jacket at me and walks up the stairs to her tower.

Flashing her pussy at me with each step.

CHAPTER SIX

He doesn't follow me immediately. It takes him a second to pull himself together.

But he does follow me. There was no chance he wouldn't.

I saw the way he looked at me. I knew what he's thinking. The same thing they all think. _Lyssa is a little prize. A little princess prize to be had. Stolen, kept, owned._

That's all anyone ever sees these days.

So he can tell himself anything he wants. He can pretend I'm not a woman, just a little girl. And that's fine.

It's just not true and the only person who needs to know this fact is me. That's all. _Never forget, Lyssa. Never forget that you're not what they think and the only opinion about you that matters is yours._

I reach the top first, his boots thudding on the hardwood stairs behind me.

"I don't trust you," he says. Like this is the reason he followed me up. I roll my eyes.

"Nor should you," I say, turning to face him as he reaches the top step and takes in my bedroom. "I wouldn't trust me either. If you think I'm just gonna go to sleep, and wake up, and magically turn back into some sweet, innocent, polite little girl—well, think again."

"What the fuck is this?" he asks.

"My room," I say. "You don't like it?"

"Yeah, well…" He laughs. "Did he decorate this room when you were six? Because…"

I look at it from his own fresh perspective. Make no mistake, it looks the same to me after all these years too. But I try to see it from the perspective of a grown man who doesn't have a thing for little girls.

White four-poster bed with a frilly canopy. Matching white dressing table with an oval mirror and a padded stool. Matching white nightstands. Fuzzy, pink rug covering the dark, hardwood floor. A little dining set that I'd pay money to see this Mason asshole sitting at, sipping tea. And a crystal chandelier hanging over the center of the tiny table.

"No," I say, matter-of-factly. "I'm pretty sure he did this back when I was eighteen when he decorated the rest of the house. If you ask him—I don't know why you would, but maybe you'll have a conversation with him tomorrow and the subject comes up—but if you ask him he'll say it's for my daughter. Future daughter, that is."

"Ah," Mason says. Like, *She's lying.*

Which is fine. I don't care. Not even the point, anyway.

"But," I say, tracing my finger over the top of the desk. "All this was mine. Back in my old room. He just brought it here." I pull open the desk drawer and find it full of crap. I laugh a little. "See?" I ask him. "My stuff. All my old stuff is in here."

"So," he says, picking up a teddy bear off the dresser, then putting it down just as quick. "Anyway. I just need to get through a few more hours with you and then I'm out of here. So. Like I said, I don't trust you."

"Do you want the bed?" I ask. "Or the beanbag?"

He laughs uncomfortably as he looks at the pink beanbag in the far corner.

It matches the rug.

He sighs. Loudly. Like he didn't ask for this and maybe he could just lock me up here and wait downstairs.

Oh, no, Mr. Mason Whatever-your-name-is. You're not getting off that easy.

You kidnapped me tonight. You fucked with my life. And now… I'm gonna fuck with yours back.

"What's wrong?" I coo, stepping towards him.

Those brilliant green eyes of his catch mine and hold.

I know he wants me. I have that effect on men. I know what he saw when I walked up the stairs naked in front of him.

I know what I'm doing. I know exactly what I'm doing.

Too bad he doesn't. Not yet.

I know how to play with a man.

When I reach him—he didn't move—I reach up and feel the fabric of his blue button-down shirt collar, then direct my eyes up to his without tilting my head. "You're not afraid of little bratty me, are you?"

"Look, Lyssa," he says, grabbing my wrist and pushing my hand away. "I know what you're doing."

"So?" I say, swaying my shoulders a little to make him look at my tits. "Does it matter if I'm seducing you?"

"You're not—"

"Or… are you one of those men who likes to do the seducing?"

"—seducing me."

I smile and blink my eyes. Then walk over to the bed. It's a high four-poster. So when I bend over and place my breasts on the mattress, my ass is up in the air. "Spank me again."

"What?"

"You heard me. Spank me again. I know you like it. I like it too. And I'm going to be bad, so if you don't do it, I'll just *make* you do it."

He just looks at me.

Oh, poor, poor Mason. You have no idea what you walked into, do you?

"Do I have to swear?" I ask. "To make you do it? Like last time? Hmmm? Or should I just beg you to fuck me?"

"Just… knock it off, OK? Why do you have to be so—"

"So *what?*" I snap. Sick of him. Sick of everything. "So defiant? So bossy? So incorrigible?"

I reach around, grab my ass with both hands, and spread my cheeks open for him.

"What the fuck?" he says.

I laugh into the bedspread, then let go of my ass, stand back up, and twirl to meet his gaze again. "God, you're like all the rest. Weak," I say. "Stupid," I say. "Selfish."

"You know what?" he says.

"What?" I coo, walking towards him again. I reach for his shirt collar, and this time, when he grabs my wrist, I fight it. Not hard, but hard enough for him to get the message that I'm not gonna let go unless he really puts some effort in to it.

"You're fucking crazy, you know that?"

I smile. He smiles.

Then I slap his face and say, "Don't use that language in front of me."

Two seconds later he's spun me around, marched me over to the bed, and has me over his knee.

"You want a fucking spanking?" he asks, grabbing my hair and pulling my head up so I have to arch my back as I'm forced to look him in the face.

I don't say anything now. Now is when the show gets interesting and I know what part I play.

He slaps my ass hard. Too hard. Much harder than he did previously. I yelp and it's not even fake.

"You're a dirty little slut," he says. "No wonder your stepfather had you kidnapped. You're not only a danger to yourself, you're a fucking danger to society."

He smacks me again. Even harder. "Shit!" I say.

Another smack. "Don't you use that fucking language with me, you little whore."

Smack!

"Ow!" I say. Because holy hell, he's not playing. He's really fucking hitting me.

Smack!

I struggle this time. Trying to squirm my way off him.

"Not so fun anymore, is it, Lyssa?"

"Stop it!" I say.

"What? I'm not playing by your rules? Honey, I don't know where you got the impression that I'm anything other than a man who *breaks* the rules, but that was a mistake."

And then his fingers slip between my legs and begin caressing my pussy.

I moan a little. My ass is still hot and stinging from his spankings.

His other hand comes down hard on the other cheek. The one he hasn't been hitting, so it's a fresh burst of pain.

"Stop it!" I yell.

He grabs my hair, pulls me off his lap, shoves me down on my knees in front of him, and says, "Make me."

I'm breathing heavy. My tits heaving up and down with each panting breath. I stare up at him. Those green eyes and that hard jaw.

And then I reach for his belt.

Never taking my eyes off him as I unbuckle it, pop the button, pull the zipper down, and reach inside to find…

"What the fuck is this?" I laugh. Because he's wearing a fucking cup. Jesus. My stepfather really did tell him what to expect.

"Good thing I had that on earlier," he says, grinning like a boy.

I just smirk at him. "Well, you gonna take it off? Or what? I can't give you a blow job while you're wearing a cup."

He shakes his head at me. "You're not gonna blow me. That's a privilege you didn't earn yet."

"Is that so?" I laugh. But hey. Point to Mason for that little comeback. Well done.

"Lyssa," he says, staring me dead in the eyes. "I don't know what game you *think* you're playing, but whatever it is, that's not the one I'm gonna win tonight."

I huff some air. Whatever.

So I just sit back on my butt, even though he's still got a firm grip on my hair and I have to bend my neck down to do that, and place both my hands on my thighs. "Tell me what to do then."

"No," he says. "You're fucking crazy. And I'm not. I'm not gonna get mixed up with you."

"Oh?" I laugh, tossing my head back so far, he either has to pull my hair really hard or let go. He lets go. "I'm crazy? I'm the crazy one here? Why don't you retrace your steps yesterday, Mr. Psycho. Play back all the decisions you made and how you ended up here, in my bedroom, with me naked and on my knees in front of your unzipped pants, and then… *then* we can talk about who's crazy."

He stands up and starts to walk away.

"Wait," I say, grabbing on to his leg. He stops, but doesn't turn to look at me. "Just… touch me then. The way you just were."

He looks over his shoulder at me and says, in a very deep, low growly voice, "How was I just touching you?"

Oh, I get it. He wants me to dirty-talk him. Or maybe talk him into this?

I do admit, he's got some real self-control in his arsenal. Not many men would be able to resist my invitation. Curiosity bubbles up inside me like the fizzy inside a bottle of champagne. And then, like the cork that has to pop, it explodes into action.

"Bend me over your knee again and stick your fingers in my pussy," I whisper, my eyes locked with his. They are very beautiful eyes. Green, but the outer edge of his irises are dark. Almost black. And the green isn't all the same color, either. It's lighter right up against the dark ring, leaning a little towards yellow. Which makes him look a little surreal. I wait a beat and then whisper, "*Please.*"

He shakes his head. "No. You're drawing me into some bratty-little-rich-girl plot. Some seriously fucked-up plot and I'm not gonna fall for it."

"You're going to be gone in a few hours," I say. "What do you care? You know you want to or you wouldn't have done it." I spin around on the rug and open my legs for him.

"You really are a little fucking slut."

I slip my fingers between my legs and begin to rub myself. Caressing my pussy the way he was just a minute ago. Then I close my eyes and hope for the best.

He hesitates. I start counting. And when I get to three, he's sitting on the bed again.

"Lie over my knee," he says.

I swallow hard and force myself not to smile as I stand up and place myself over his legs.

CHAPTER SEVEN

I hold my breath as she places her perfect, plump ass over my knee. Her elbows are propped up on the mattress, her head bowed into her hands like she's praying. Her feet are still on the floor, so she's kind of half in and half out of my lap, but I'm not going to get picky here.

Lyssa Baylor is lying across my lap, begging me to spank her.

That held breath comes out with a smile.

Oh, you filthy little slut. No wonder your daddy wants you married off as soon as possible. Unexpectedly, I feel a little jealous. Not sure about what. That she's a horny little whore? Or that she's getting married?

Probably neither. Probably this is just due to the fact that I'm hard, wearing a cup, and there's no way I can fuck this girl. Not tonight, not ever.

I'd really like to. Like… *really* like to.

But no. I won't. I'm gonna spank her until she comes then go down to a bathroom, spank my own monkey, get her out of my head, and be ready to get the fuck out of here when her stepfather shows up.

My hand hovers over the bright pink handprints emblazoned on her ass cheeks. I need a picture before I leave. That will be my reward for not fucking her.

I place my hand on her ass, rubbing it back and forth across the smooth creamy skin. She wiggles it a little bit, trying to entice me.

I want to tell her that's not how this will work. That I have more self-control than any man she's ever met in her baby princess life. I have had my patience tested in ways she can't even imagine. And I will not touch her without thinking things through first.

She wiggles again. Anticipating the smack that never comes.

"Little baby princess," I say.

She kinda looks over her shoulder at me. Bites her lip. "What?" she whispers.

"If you wiggle your ass one more time, trying to turn me on without my permission, I will walk out and never touch you again. I will lock you up here, pay no attention to you at all, and then leave without saying goodbye."

She glares at me. "You *would* do that, wouldn't you?"

"Try me," I say. "And find out."

She looks away, shifting her feet a little. Then she looks back and says, "I wasn't wiggling. It's just… this is a weird position to be in and I'm uncomfortable."

"Aww," I say, petting her ass, rubbing my palm across her skin in small soft circles. "Is the little princess uncomfortable? Poor thing."

She sucks in a breath of air, bites her lip again, then exhales as she bows her head back down into her hands on the mattress.

I smile. She is much calmer now than she was a few minutes ago. So I continue to rub my hand all over her ass. Enjoying the feel of her soft skin. My palm does small circles over the underside of her ass, then my fingertips just barely graze down the back of her thigh to the dent behind her knee.

"Oh, God," she moans.

"Do you like that?" I ask.

"I thought you were gonna save me."

"What?"

"Spank me, I mean." She shakes her head. "I don't know why I said that. I meant spank me."

"I'm trying to get you calm. I think it's working."

"Why?" she asks. "Why bother getting me calm when you're just gonna wind me up again?"

Because I fucking feel like it.

That's what I want to say, and it's the truth. But it feels a little selfish and unnecessary for her first real moment of submission. So I put a little more thought into it.

"Why calm you down if I'm just gonna wind you up? Well, I think the dynamic between pain and pleasure is interesting and it intrigues me. Also..." This thought just occurs to me, right this second. "I think it's been a long time since you were calm. I think it's probably a bit of a relief. So I'm doing you a favor."

She sucks in another breath of air, holds it for a moment, then lets it out.

I think she lets out a lot of things with that breath. Stress, for sure. Because I feel her body relax in my lap. Her breathing evens out, and her head tilts to the side. One cheek facing me, eye closed, mouth closed. Like she might fall asleep.

She could probably use some sleep. It's been a wild night and things are only going to get worse for her soon. So I decide not to spank her, but reward her for giving in, instead.

I drag the backs of my fingertips up and down the back of her thigh. Sometimes stopping when I get to her knee, sometimes continuing down her calf as far as I can reach.

If she were truly lying across my lap her legs would be up on the mattress and then I could caress her calf and tickle the soles of her feet.

I smile and think, *Yeah, I'm gonna do that next time.*

But then I realize there's not going to be a next time. This is it.

I don't want to reposition her though. She's content, and quiet, and maybe even asleep.

My hand sweeps up her leg, grabs one cheek of her ass, and then I slip the underside of my hand down between her legs. All four fingers playing with her pussy while my thumb caresses small circles around her asshole.

"Oh," she moans softly. Eyes still closed.

I smile, but don't say anything. I truly do not want to disturb her. Her falling asleep while I make her come is the ideal outcome here.

Two of my fingers find her clit. The other two slip inside her pussy.

She is very wet. Wet enough that they slip in and out without much resistance.

I lean forward, place my lips on her ass cheek, and then kiss it.

She moans sleepily.

Damn. She might be being a little too good.

Or maybe I'm just being too soft.

Oh, well. Let her remember me as that one guy who slowed her down and made stillness feel amazing.

Her legs begin to tremble and when I look down I realize she's been standing on her tiptoes this whole time. Straining to maintain position.

"Lyssa," I say.

"Hmmm?" she mumbles.

"Climb on to the bed, lie face down, and spread your legs. I'll give you what you want and then you're gonna go to sleep and forget about this day. Understand me?"

She takes a deep breath, lifts her head up—her disheveled hair falling over her face—and nods as she climbs off me and crawls across the bed.

She collapses onto the covers, grabs the pillow with both hands, and then points her toes and opens her legs.

Which makes me hold in a laugh, but not a smile.

So dramatic, little baby princess.

I stand up, crawl across the bed, both my hands on her ass cheeks, spreading them wide as I lean down to lick her.

"Oh, God," she says.

Oh, God is right. I'm so fucking hard, I can't stand this cup anymore. I reach inside my boxer briefs, pull the cup out, then push my pants and underwear down until my cock is free.

When I look back at Lyssa, she's staring at me.

"No," I say, shaking my head. "This is not for you, sweet baby. This is just for me."

She closes her eyes, shaking her head. But obviously too tired to care.

I stretch my legs out on her bed, my face deep between her legs—licking and swirling my tongue around her clit—while I pull and tug on my fat, stiff cock. Fisting it hard.

The pussy licking is good for her. But not enough. I can't come until she does, and I really want to come, so I need a way to get her off quick.

I sit up on my knees, still jerking myself with one hand while the other one slips back into position. Two fingers on her clit, two inside her pussy, and my thumb on her asshole.

I push my thumb inside—just a little—and make her moan. I wonder if she's ever had anal? God, I'd like to be first, if she hasn't.

Jesus, Mason. You're leaving in like three hours and you'll never see this girl again.

Right. I keep forgetting that for some reason.

Her knees come up, spreading her pussy open for me a little more. "Please," she says. "Put it inside me."

"You don't need my cock, baby princess. Just enjoy my fingers."

"No, it's not enough."

"Oh, I think it is."

"Mason—"

Holy hell. Hearing her say my name kinda turns me on. "Roll over on your stomach," I say.

She maneuvers her legs so I don't have to change position, then turns over—eyes locked on mine—and lifts up her knees as she opens her legs wide.

I take a peek at her pussy. All wet with her juices. And decide how to make her come.

"Scoot over a little," I say, crawling up the side of her body. This ridiculous canopy bed is twin-sized, so we barely fit. My body alone barely fits, so it's a good thing she's tiny and I'm lying on my side.

Her hand reaches for my cock but I brush it away, then flick her nipple with my fingers and say, "Don't touch me without permission."

She huffs, but stays silent. On her knees, ass in the air.

"You just be still and enjoy it, OK?"

"I thought you were punishing me? Doesn't sound like punishment."

"Well…" She's right. I'm totally off script here. "Enjoy it anyway."

I begin slowly. Rubbing all four fingers around in a circle over her clit. She begins to breathe heavy. Panting like a wild animal. And when I pick up speed— rubbing those circles faster, then faster, then even faster—her knees come up and squeeze together, like I'm overwhelming her.

"Oh… I can't… shit… Mason… My God…"

It really fucking turns me on.

And her too. Because when I stick two fingers back inside her pussy and begin to pump in and out so hard her whole body is jerking with the momentum, she squirts her delicious juice all over my hand. It leaks down between her ass cheeks and all over her pretty princess bedspread.

I pull my hand away, get up on my knees, and fist my throbbing cock several times, and then shoot my come all over her tits. Moaning and groaning with relief. She reaches for my cock, her body still convulsing from her climax, and I'm so distracted by how good this all feels, I don't brush it away.

She pumps out the rest of my come. Her small hand barely fitting around my shaft.

I close my eyes until I'm finished. She leans forward, swipes the tip of her tongue around my head, then puts me inside her mouth.

Oh. Fuck.

No, no, no. We're done here. What I did was wrong on so many levels. Every fucking minute I've been with this girl has been wrong. The drugging, the fight in the alley, the van ride, the house, the bedroom, and now this.

I'm one fucked-up dude.

I push her head back, then get up off the bed, tuck my dick away, and walk downstairs.

If she were really mine I would stay. I want to tell her that so she doesn't think I left for the wrong reasons. She's so messed up, what I just did tonight could make her worse and I suddenly feel bad for walking out.

I could go up there and try to explain myself. Turn it into something lighter. Like… I'd hold her all night and make her feel safe but that goddamned bed isn't big enough for two grownups. It was made for a single little princess.

She might even laugh. It could even make her relax a little and fall asleep. Knowing that I'm not as bad as I seem.

Because I'm really not. I'm not this guy at all, actually. I just… need that fucking money her stepfather promised me. It's really important that I get it. And I'm sorry she's the way I get that done, but…

Fuck it.

I don't go back up there. I don't tell her any of that.

After cleaning up in the bathroom I pull a chair into the hallway at the bottom of her stairs, and listen for the sound of tires on the gravel driveway outside that will announce the arrival of her stepfather and the end of my time with Lyssa Baylor.

CHAPTER EIGHT

I wake up to the sound of a luxury car door closing outside. "Fuck," I grumble. "He's here."

But then I remember what happened last night. Well, most of it. The ride in the van is still pretty hazy.

Mason though. He's not hazy at all.

God. Why did we have to meet like this? He's not what I expected. And yeah, it's fucked up on so many Stockholm syndrome levels that I'm thinking about him like this, but I don't care.

I just have a feeling about him.

If we had met somewhere else, if we had met on a different night and under different circumstances, I would like him. He's rough and controlling, but not in a bad way. Not the way I've experienced it with men before.

And yes, I do realize that I was drugged, kidnapped, stripped naked, spanked, and maybe a little bit humiliated—but… it wasn't personal.

It wasn't me making him do that stuff. It was my stepfather. But I get this feeling that's not really why he's here, either. He's not the typical man my stepfather employs. A memory of him talking to my stepfather on the phone last night in the van flashes though my head.

I told you my terms. I'll be there in three hours and you had better be waiting. I'm a bounty hunter, not a goddamned babysitter.

He gave my stepfather an *order*.

Who does that?

This guy Mason, apparently.

I reach down between my legs and find the sheets still damp, then realize I nodded off right after he left my room. Didn't even bother to clean myself up. So there's dried come all over my breasts.

I force myself up, jump in the shower, and clean myself up. I will be presentable for the next phase of my stepfather's plan. I need to get out of here. I need to be rational, and sane, and think clearly or…

I don't want to think about that.

There are clothes in my closet because of course there are. I choose a white cotton eyelet dress that makes me look like a six-year-old going to a garden party and not a twenty-five-year-old being sentenced to confinement before my forced wedding to stupid Dickerson.

They are already talking downstairs in the office when I descend the left side of the grand staircase barefoot.

I stop at the bottom and listen to the conversation, safely hidden from sight.

"No," Mason says. He sounds angry. I take a few steps closer, trying to figure out why. "I told you. Wire transfer only."

"Well, I'm sorry," my stepfather says. "I can't do it right now."

"You better be able to fucking do it. I kidnapped your daughter outside a club. I put myself at risk and still delivered the goods."

Goods. I huff. *Thanks a lot, Mason whoever-you-are. It's every girl's dream to be referred to as goods.* Still, he's the only chance I have. I showed him the bedroom and planted all the right seeds in his head. Now… what will he do with that information?

"So you're gonna hold up your end, Mr. Baylor."

"Or what?" my stepfather challenges. I creep a few steps closer, getting a look at them through the French doors that lead into the office.

"I don't make threats," Mason says. His shirt is untucked and his hair is mussed up and sexy from all our various interactions last night.

"Oh, Lyssa," my stepfather says, spying me spying on them. "There you are." He smiles at me. "You look well." Then he tilts his head. "Are you well?"

I take a few more steps, see another man standing in the office—someone I don't know but who looks a lot like an accountant, if I had to make an assumption—and enter the office so I can be closer to Mason one last time before he leaves.

"I'm fine," I say, letting out a long breath with the words.

"Good," my stepfather says. "This is Mr. Lanrey," he says, pointing to the accountant.

"So?" I say. Fully aware that was rude, but not caring. Because Mr. Lanrey is looking at me with disgust. Or maybe contempt. Or possibly true revulsion.

"He's your tutor," my stepfather explains. Saying the words slowly like I'm challenged in the area of understanding the English language.

I am instantly a million more times irritated than I was two seconds ago. "Tutor for what?" I snap. "Does getting married to Dickerson Worthington require some kind of entrance exam? Because if so, I think I'll fail on purpose."

My stepfather scowls at me. "Why do you always act this way?"

"Why do *you* always act this way?" I snarl back. "You hired someone to drug me. Kidnap me. Drag me here, even though I didn't want to come, and you knew I didn't want to come."

"You're marrying that boy. You've known that for over a year now. You accepted his ring. You are not calling this off."

"Or what?" I challenge him the way he just did Mason.

"You know what," he responds. Then he turns to the accountant and says, "Take her somewhere. Anywhere. Just get her out of my sight."

Lanrey comes towards me, reaching for my arm. But I take a step back and say, in the calmest voice I can muster—because everything depends on being calm right now—"Do not. *Touch me.*"

"Miss Baylor," Lanrey says. He's tall, and kinda skinny. He could be a waiter at a fancy restaurant, maybe. He's kinda dressed like that. "Please," he says, folding his hands at his waist and leaning forward a little, as if in a bow. "Take me on a tour of the home so I can get acclimated."

"Tour of the home?" I ask, raising one eyebrow at my stepfather.

"He'll be staying here with you until the wedding. I've hired him to change you from an unruly, wild brat into a compliant, obedient wife."

"Is that so?" I ask, continuing to raise that one eyebrow.

I don't even bother looking at Mason for help. He's clearly had enough and my dreamy feelings about him have suddenly faded. He's got one foot out the door, as they say. Whatever disagreement he's having with my stepfather over money will be sorted and then he'll be satisfied and leave. He'll forget all about me.

And why should I care? For real, why? He's just another stranger in a long line of people my stepfather has brought in and out of my life since I was six.

Just another employee who sees something and decides not to *say* something because of my last name.

"And," I add, picking back up with the conversation I'm having with my asshole stepfather, "what if I don't want to be a compliant, obedient wife? What then? Is there an option B hiding behind door number two?"

"No," my stepfather says, turning to look down at his open briefcase on the office desk. Like the matter is now closed.

But is the matter closed?

I think not.

So I turn and smile at the waiter who might be an accountant. "I'd be delighted to show you around, Mr. Lanrey."

Then I do a little curtsey.

Lanrey blushes, chuckles, then looks at my stepfather. Like maybe my good-girl manners just got him hard and now he's not quite sure what to do.

"Go ahead," my stepfather says. "I have business with Mr. Macintyre."

Macintyre. Holy shit. The hot kidnapper's name is Mason *Macintyre.*

It's quite nice. Quite sexy too. It's like his parents asked themselves, *What name could we possibly give our new boy child that will make him irresistible to every woman ever?*

Whew. That was it. Good choice, Mr. and Mrs. Macintyre.

The only way to make this guy hotter is to put him on a fire truck decked out in fireman gear.

I wonder what his job title is?

Princess hunter?

That almost makes me laugh.

"Lyssa?" my stepfather says.

"What?"

"Stop daydreaming. Mr. Lanrey is waiting for you."

Right. Him.

OK, Lyssa. Let's do this.

I take a deep breath, walk over to Mr. Lanrey—who is waiting just outside the office door—place both hands on his shoulders, grip his suit coat tight, and knee him in the balls.

"Ugggghhhhhhhhhh!" Lanrey moans. "Oh, my fuuuuuuuuuck! My fuuuccccccckkk-kkiiiiingg *GOD!*"

It's a really terrible moan too. Like… not one becoming of a gentleman who dresses like an accountant-slash-waiter and is hired to turn wild princesses into demure ladies.

My stepfather comes storming through the office, pushes me away from Lanrey so hard, I fall to the floor and hit my head, and then starts making excuses for me.

"I'm sorry. I'm so sorry. She's… you see why we need you. She's just so wild and out of control, and—"

I stop listening because Mason is picking me up off the floor. "You OK?" he asks.

I suck in a deep breath, trying to get a handle on the adrenaline flooding through my body, but that makes me start to shake.

I let out that breath and say, "I'm fine," as I brush his hand off my arm.

"No," Mason says. "You're bleeding." And then he swipes a fingertip over the back of my head and shows me blood. "Does it hurt?" he asks.

"What do you think?" I ask, taking a step away from him.

"Hey," he says, taking hold of my arm again and gripping it tight. "I'm on your side, OK?"

"Are you sure about that?" I ask him. "Because you're on *his* payroll."

We both look at my stepfather, who is staring at us. Watching our interaction.

"I'm afraid I can't do this," Lanrey says. "I knew your daughter was a troubled child, and I've worked with many troubled young ladies. But she's the first to physically attack me."

I growl at him, baring my teeth. *Wild Thing.*

Mason growls back, shaking me by the arm. "Knock it off, Lyssa. Just stand still and be good."

My stepfather is shaking his head. "Mr. Lanrey, you've already been paid—"

"He's been paid?" Mason says. "He didn't even do his job. Why haven't *I* been paid?"

"You'll get your money, Mr. Macintyre," my stepfather says, then turns back to Lanrey. "Mr. Lanrey, as I stated—"

"Consider yourself refunded," Lanrey says, glaring at me. His face is all red and his eyes are still watering. "I do not work with animals."

Hmmm. Well, there you go. I'm an animal.

"Your car can take me back to the city now," he says, then walks to the front door and pulls on it.

I smile. I know I shouldn't. I know it's inappropriate, especially when I just humiliated this man. But I don't care. I smile because he's locked in and the door doesn't budge.

And then I start giggling at the irony. Giggling like a stupid little schoolgirl who smoked pot on her way to class and is now having a fit.

"Stop it," Mason grows at me. He's still holding on to my upper arm, so he tugs on it again.

"I'm sorry," I say, smiling at him. "It's kinda funny though, right? They lock me in and then he's—" I giggle again.

"Lyssa, I'm not going to repeat myself," Mason hisses. "*Shut. Up.*"

I huff out a sigh and make a face at him. "I don't have a lot of joy in my life, OK? Why can't I laugh when I find something funny?"

"Because you're laughing at his expense, that's why. Jesus Christ. Who the fuck raised you?"

Everyone looks at my stepfather. He tilts his chin up, then sucks in a deep breath of air, walks over to the door, and unlocks it.

Lanrey rushes through like I'm gonna chase him down like a wild dog.

I almost laugh again, but Mason Macintyre is on to me now because he preemptively whispers, "Don't you dare, princess. Don't you *dare.*"

"Lyssa," my stepfather says, looking at us in again. "Go upstairs to your room."

I yank my arm out of Mason's grip and say, "Go fuck yourself," to my stepfather.

But I do leave. And I do go upstairs.

But I do not go to my room.

Baylor walks to the office door and says, "Mr. Macintyre, please. Come into the office."

"So we can discuss my *payment*, I hope," I say under my breath.

"You're going to get paid. I told you, I have cash. You're the one who refused it."

"Because I don't need cash, Baylor. I need a fucking wire transfer."

"You can transfer it—"

"Look," I say, losing patience with this asshole. "We made these terms. I explained them to you when I accepted the job. I have my reasons and you don't need to know why I want a wire transfer instead of cash, OK? This is just how it is. So transfer the fucking money."

"It's Sunday," he says.

"So what?"

"I only do transfers through my bank so it won't go through until tomorrow anyway. I don't understand what the big deal is?"

"The big deal is you didn't take me fucking seriously. You came here with cash—"

"I made a mistake," Baylor says. "I apologize for that. OK?" He spreads his hands out in a mea culpa.

I don't say anything. I'm too angry. I was counting on that transfer going through last night and now I find out it didn't. So I think I'm justifiably pissed off.

"But since you're already here, how would you like to make a little more money?"

I shake my head and laugh.

"I mean to say a lot more money. I'll pay you double what I paid Lanrey."

"Yeah? How much was that?"

"Two hundred and fifty thousand."

Well… that makes me shut the fuck up.

Baylor smiles. Because he knows he's got my attention.

"You paid that asshole a hundred and twenty-five thousand to what? Tame your daughter?"

"No, you misunderstood. I paid *him* two fifty. *You* I will pay five hundred."

"What the hell? Why would you—"

But he cuts me off by making a stop motion with his hand. "Just as I do not need to know your business, Mr. Macintyre, you do not need to know mine."

I shake my head again. "No. No, I'm afraid I'm not interested in being part of your sick daddy-daughter plans."

He laughs a little. "Sick? What?"

"She showed me her bedroom. That's pretty fucked up."

"What are you talking—" Then he sighs. "Oh. OK. I get it. She told you that story, did she?"

I narrow my eyes at him. "Which story?"

"The one where I make her sleep in a child's bedroom? Did she tell you I decorated that princess room for her?"

I don't say anything. Which is the answer he was expecting.

"I see," he says. "Would you like to come with me?"

"Why?"

"Because I'd like to show you something."

"Show me what?"

"Just indulge me, Mr. Macintyre. Please. I've had a very trying morning and it would be wonderful if I could get someone to cooperate." He walks over to the door and waves his hand, beckoning me to come forward.

"I'm pretty sick of the games," I say. But I go with him over to the stairs. We walk up the closest staircase and stop on the second floor.

He points to the end of the hallway where the princess room is hidden behind the closed double doors. "That room," he says, "is for my future grandchildren."

"So I've heard," I grumble.

"Yes, I'm sure she told you quite a story. But did she show you all the rooms? Or just that one?"

"I saw a few of them."

He walks down to a closed door, one we didn't peek into last night, and opens it wide. "Go ahead, take a look."

God, these people are fucking weird. But I go to the door and walk into the room.

It's a little boy's room. Sports theme. Big Fathead stickers of pro ballplayers on the wall. Blue and orange-themed color. Twin bed. The kind with a bunch of drawers underneath. A desk with a football light.

"There's more," Baylor says. Walking down the hallway. I follow him and he opens another door we didn't look into.

A nursery. Neutral yellow on the walls. White crib, teddy bear mobile hanging over it. Changing table, rocking chair, and a toy box filled with toys.

"I know what she told you. Or at the very least, what she implied. You aren't the first person she's lied to about me, Mr. Macintyre. She is the most manipulative, selfish, out-of-control young lady I've ever seen in my life. And yes, I raised her. So maybe I turned her into that. Or maybe…" he says, lowering his voice as he stares down the hall.

I turn to follow his gaze and see Lyssa down the hallway. Leaning against an open door like she hasn't got a care in the world.

"Or maybe," he continues. "She was just born that way."

I look back at him.

"She was a difficult child and now she's a very disturbed young woman. And she's gotten herself into a lot of trouble over the years. I have a whole file of her police record down in that office. It was for Lanrey, but you're welcome to read it. I am only trying to help her. And this marriage? It's good for her," he says. "It will be helpful for her to have structure in her life. To be here, in this house. One that is hers and hers alone. And to have a man like Dickerson Worthington beside her, keeping her steady and straight. He is steady, Mason. He is straight. And my daughter needs that more than you can comprehend right now."

I cringe a little when he uses my first name. Because it changes our relationship somehow.

"She will tell you he's boring, but he's just calm. There is nothing wrong with being calm. She's just been running wild for so long, she's lost her way. And ever since her mother died two years ago, she's only gotten worse. That's why we set up the marriage. And she agreed to it. Make no mistake about that. She took his ring and told him yes. But… she's gotten worse over the past several months. Much, much worse. The toll of her mother's death has changed her in ways that might not be reversible if she doesn't get help and settle down. She needs that, Mason. She needs help. So I'm begging you. *Help her.* It's clear that the two of you formed a bond over this little abduction job. She listened to you down there. But more than that, she *wanted* to listen to you. I will not only have your wire transfer of fifty thousand dollars for last night's job go through first thing tomorrow morning, I will add half a million more to that same transfer. Money up front. Just like I did for Lanrey."

He stops to frown at me. Let me take all that in.

Shit, man. Five hundred fifty thousand tax-free dollars? How do I turn that down?

"Two weeks," Baylor says. "That's it. All you have to do is keep her here. Tame her a little. Make her into the lady I know she is. And then you walk away a rich man."

"Rich?" I laugh. "That's nothing to you."

"OK," he says. "How about five *million?*"

"Fuck off," I say.

"I'm serious," he says, leaning in to me as he continues to stare at Lyssa all the way down the hall. "I need this problem solved. *Now.*"

Interesting way to put it. But I tuck that away for later consideration.

Because five million tax-free dollars really does make me rich.

But everything about this man feels dirty and wrong. Lots of parents are disappointed in their children. It's not really their business once they turn eighteen. Like… I want to tell this guy to get a life. To move on, let her go and do her thing, and forget about her.

But I already know what he'll say next.

He can't. Not when he is who he is. This important billionaire who dominates the stock reports. He can't have his daughter flashing her pussy at nightclubs and getting into trouble.

It's bad for business.

I have a lot of feelings about that. Mostly disgust, but there's a healthy dose of indifference in there too. Because I just do not relate to these people. It makes no sense to me.

My mother didn't raise me like this. We weren't poor. I wasn't bullied, I didn't grow up in a bad neighborhood or go to bad schools. It was all very middle-class average. It was all very *normal*.

And nothing about these people strikes me as anything close to normal.

"No," I say, shaking my head. "I'm sorry, Mr. Baylor. I kinda like her, and I really do wish you all the best, but... I just want my fifty grand and I'll be on my way."

He smiles at me. Except it's not a smile. Because smiles are meant to convey happiness and this isn't happiness. It's... something else.

"I know why you need that transfer, Mr. Macintyre. I do my research before I hire people to take care of sensitive situations for me."

"Sure you do," I say.

"Your mother is in Sweden. Some non-FDA approved cancer treatment?"

What the fuck?

"I know that team. She's still in the preliminary trial stage, right? Oh, it's a very promising treatment. I've heard that the last trial had some remarkable results. More than half of the patients are now cancer-free. I really do hope your mother gets accepted into the full program. Could save her life. Probably *will* save her life."

"Fuck you," I growl, low and dangerous. Because this asshole doesn't get to have an opinion about my mother's cancer, or her treatment, or her chances of survival. He hasn't earned that privilege.

"Five million dollars," he says. "Five million dollars *and* I'll make sure your mother is accepted tomorrow. I'm sorry the wire transfer will be late, but it won't matter once I make a simple phone call."

This motherfucker did this on purpose. To get my mother accepted into the new trial I have to put up fifty thousand dollars to show I can support her over the next several months while she's in treatment. Baylor knew the deadline was Monday morning at nine AM Swedish time. And he came here with cash just in case his little princess-reform-school headmaster didn't work out.

He knew. He planned this down to the very last detail.

"You can call her," Baylor says. "She'll be excited. She'll want to tell you all about it."

I glare at him. "You really don't give a fuck, do you? You really have an impression of yourself."

"What impression is that? That I'm untouchable?" He laughs. "Well… I am, Mr. Macintyre. We both know what kind of power I wield. Your mother needs something and so do I." He holds his hands up like it's just that simple. "Besides, you're already in too deep to just walk away."

"You're a sick fuck, you know that?" I say.

"I have no idea what you mean. I care about my daughter. And even though I don't know your mother, I'm sure she's a very deserving woman. I'm only trying to help you help me."

It's wrong. The whole thing is wrong. The stuff with Lyssa. The blackmail with my mother.

But… she'll get the treatment. And with that money I can buy her a little house near her doctors so she doesn't have to stay in the hospital ward. So even if it doesn't work—it will, but even if it doesn't—she'll have a nice home at the end of her life.

And if I say no to this man right now? Well, it's not hard to predict that future. He'll make sure she doesn't get accepted. And then she'll die there. Or here. Doesn't matter. She *will* die.

"Are we agreed, then?" Baylor asks.

I sigh, then turn to look at Lyssa. Turn back to Baylor and nod. "Fine. It's a deal. What exactly do you expect me to do with Lyssa?"

"Force her to stop all this lying, and slutting around, and drug use. Make her into the wife Dickerson Worthington *thinks* he's getting. I might be untouchable, Mason. But you're not. Your mother isn't. And my daughter isn't either."

Then he smiles at me in a way that sends a chill up my spine. "So go ahead. Do whatever you want. Touch her all you need to. Just be sure to *break her* by the time you're done."

Neither of them say anything to me as they walk back to the stairs and descend. Something has been said. Some deal has been struck. That's all I can figure. I sit on the top step and watch them go into my stepfather's office and close the door. Close the deal too, I suppose.

About thirty minutes later, the doors open again and my stepfather walks out. He looks up at me and smiles. "Goodbye, Lyssa. See you in ten days. The event planners will arrive and begin setting up for the wedding. Your dress is in your room. Please try it on and decide if you think it needs any alterations. Then have Mason call me and let me know." He smiles wider, which just makes me want to puke. "You're going to look lovely."

Then he unlocks the front door, leaves, and locks it back up behind him.

"Well." I sigh. "I guess that's it."

When I glance back at the office, Mason is standing in the doorway. Arms folded across his chest.

"So you're in charge of me now," I say.

"Looks that way," he says.

I take in a deep breath and let it out. "Now what?"

He laughs a little. "Well… I'm not really sure, wild thing. What do you usually do with your days?"

"Sleep off a hangover."

That makes him laugh louder. "OK. Well. Do you have a hangover? Do you need to sleep?"

I think about this. Since I was out drinking last night and he did drug me. But I say, "No. Not really tired anymore."

"Well, your old man left me a boatload of cash to go shopping. You wanna go shopping?"

"Shopping?" I say.

"I didn't bring any clothes," he says, his voice deep and rumbling. Like he's the one who's tired and need a day off to sleep. "And I'm not allowed to go back to the city to get some. But there's a mall about forty minutes away. So…" He shrugs. "How about it? Wanna blow this place?"

For a second I feel like he's asking me to run away with him.

My body responds before I can stop it.

My heart beats faster with excitement.

But then he holds up something in his hand and says, "But you gotta wear this."

I squint at it. "What is it?"

"It's a tracking bracelet." He pulls out his phone and says, "I've got an app now that lets me know where you are at all times."

"Wonderful." I sigh. The possibility of running away with him evaporates. "I don't really give a fuck what we do."

"Language," he says. Same low, growly voice.

"You don't like my fucking language?" I ask.

"Don't," he warns me.

"Or what?" I ask. "You'll promise to spank me and then not fucking do it?"

Even from all the way up here I can see him raise his eyebrows. "Are you complaining about last night?"

I look down to hide my smile, then get it under control and look up again. "Not really. It's just…"

"Just what?"

"You did fucking promise."

"Lyssa," he snaps. "I'm not kidding about the language. Your stepfather wants you to behave. And he's gonna pay me a lot of money and a pretty big favor to tame you into something presentable for your wedding. So if you think I'm not going to complete that job—if you think this is gonna be just ten days of flirting and fun—then you're sadly mistaken. So stop saying 'fuck,' or 'shit,' or any other cuss word that's not appropriate for a lady of your position and rank, and be good."

"A lady of my position?" I scoff.

"You are the daughter of one of the world's richest men, Lyssa. Why can't you just be thankful and gracious about that?"

"Thankful and gracious?" I scoff again. "Are you fucking kidding me right now?"

He tilts his head at me. "Come here."

"No," I say. "If you want me, catch me."

"No," he says. "I'm not gonna chase you. You're gonna chase me."

"Really?" I laugh.

"Yeah, really. Now get down here."

"And what if I don't? Hmmmm? What then?"

"Then… then I leave. I leave, lock you in, and go shopping. Maybe I'll come back tonight. Maybe I'll come back in a week. Hell, he's already promised to wire me my money first thing in the morning. So maybe I just walk away from you and your stepfather and say, 'Fuck it. I'm done.'"

"Hmm," I say. "What if I break a window and escape while you're gone? Will my stepfather's band of mercenaries come stop me?" I smile, because I know he was lying about that.

"No. The windows are actually shatterproof. But you can give it your best."

"Nice try." I laugh.

He picks a silver candlestick up off a nearby table and hurls it at the closest window. There's a loud bang, but the window does not break.

He smiles, proud of his little display. "Like I said, your choice. But in ten seconds I'm gonna take that decision away from you and then I'm gonna leave and never come back."

Do I want to be here alone? Not really. But I could handle it. It's no big deal.

"Ten," he says, counting down.

But the real question is… do I want him to leave?

And that is a firm no. Mason Macintyre might be the most interesting thing to ever happen to me. And even though he drugged me, abducted me, spanked me, and then made me squirt all over the bed, and his hand, and myself—I liked it. All of it.

So when he gets to the count of three, I stand up and walk down. He adds a zero at the end of his countdown so I'm standing in front of him just in time.

And you know what that says about him?

That he's fair.

And that's a nice change from most of the people I've been around my whole life.

"I'm on your side," he says, fastening the tracker to my wrist.

I want to say, *I know.* Because I really do think he is. But then I'd start having hopes and maybe even dreams. And if there's one thing I've learned about being Lyssa Baylor, it's that I'm not allowed to have my own hopes and dreams. They're dangerous things.

So I say nothing.

His hand reaches for my face and I flinch away on instinct.

"Don't do that," he says.

My heart begins to beat faster when I look up into his green eyes. But I close them when he brushes the back of his knuckles down my cheek.

"If we're gonna do this," he says, "you need to trust me, OK?"

I shake my head no. Eyes still closed. Because trust is a dangerous thing too. "I don't even know what we're doing," I say.

"We're taming you, Lyssa Baylor. The people who love you want me to banish that wild thing inside you."

I open my eyes and look at him. Sigh. Long and loud. I wish it were a sigh of relief, but it's not. It's resignation. The devil you know or some shit like that. It might even be surrender.

"OK?" he says, gently swiping a piece of my hair and tucking it behind my ear. "I like you without makeup," he says. "You're very pretty. You don't even need it." Then his fingers drop down to my breast, the tips feeling the soft cotton eyelet lace. "And I like this look too."

"What look?" I huff. "Six-year-old girl look?"

He smiles. "It's just simple and pretty, that's all."

That's what he sees? Because that's not what I see.

"OK," he says. "OK. I think we're on the same page now. So I would like you to walk over to the piano, bend over, lift up your dress, and then place your elbows on the keys.”

“What?” I say, looking over at the grand piano in the sunroom just off the foyer.

“I think you heard me,” he says. “And I don’t like to repeat myself.”

“But why? I did what you asked.”

“No,” he says. So calm. So gentle. “You pushed my buttons, Lyssa. So you do have to be punished for that. I can’t let anything slip, you understand, right? They don’t call you Wild Thing for nothing. So please, do as I asked.”

I try not to blush but I don’t succeed. So I turn away before he can see that. Because the thought of Mason Macintyre spanking me again gets me hot all over, not just in my face.

When I get myself under control, I turn back to him. He’s not smiling. Not frowning. In fact, there’s almost no emotion at all on his face.

Well, no, that’s not true. There is something there. I just can’t put my finger on it.

“OK?” he asks.

I want to say it’s kindness. Or no. That’s probably too strong of a word. Thoughtfulness, maybe. Or consideration. Which is a nice change from the emotion I typically get from my stepfather. Which is—

"Hello?" he says, pulling me out of my thoughts and back to him.

I swallow hard then nod my head. A few seconds later I'm in the sunroom bending over the piano. I reach behind me and lift up my dress.

"Lyssa," Mason says. "No underwear?"

"What?" I say. "I never wear underwear. What's the big deal?"

"That's fine," he says. "If you're wearing *pants*. But a lady always wears underwear in a dress. Don't do it again."

"I don't even own underwear."

"I'll get you some when we go shopping. Now elbows, please."

I smack my elbows down on the keys with a musical bang and hang my head. Anticipating his hand on my ass as my pussy begins to throb.

He walks up behind me, his fingertips brushing gently along the curve of my ass, and then I hear the sound of his belt buckle.

Oh, God. He's gonna fuck me into compliance. This whole deal is starting to look up. I bite my lip to stop the smile. Getting stuck in this house with Mason Macintyre might be the best thing ever.

But then he pulls his belt through the loop of his pants and snaps it.

I look over my shoulder and he's got a wild gleam in his eyes now, that maybe-kindness and calmness gone.

"What are you doing?" I ask.

He hits me with the belt.

Hard.

So hard I scream and turn around.

He shakes his head.

"*What* are you doing?" I demand.

"How many times did you say fuck when you were at the top of the stairs?"

"What?"

"Five, Lyssa. It was five. So you have four more beatings coming."

"Beatings?" I say, shocked. "You're going to beat me into submission?"

"That's right."

"Fuck you," I snarl. "You're not hitting me with that belt ever again." My voice is shaky and I hate that. But I can't stop it. My body is alive with adrenaline.

"Turn around. You're up to five again."

"No," I say. "No."

He starts putting his belt on again. Notices my confused face. "I do need your permission to punish you. You do have a choice here. But I also have a choice. And if you don't want to play by my rules then I'm leaving and not coming back. Ever. I don't need this, Lyssa. My mother is in Sweden dying of cancer. That's why I needed this money. I'd much rather be there with her than here with an ungrateful bratty princess who only thinks in the moment and has no regard for consequences. So decide. Because I've got better places to go, better things to do, and better people to be with."

"What?" I say, trying to unpack all those words he just threw at me.

"I'm gonna count down from three this time. Three. Two."

I spin around and bend over. Lift my dress up and plunk my elbows down on the keys. "Fine," I yell. "I choose you."

Because… because his mother is dying. And he's handsome. And he talks to me like I'm a real person and no one has *ever* done that with me.

Smack. "Ow!" I scream, tears in my eyes.

Smack. I start sobbing from the sting. There has to be a welt on my ass.

Smack. I lean my head down on the keys.

Smack. I make fists with my hands and start coughing from the pain.

Smack. My legs are shaking. I think the welts are actually bleeding.

He puts his arms around me and picks me up like a small child. Walks me through the foyer and into the great room. Then sets me on my feet, sits down on the couch, and says, "Lie over my knee."

"No more," I beg. It hurts so bad I can barely think.

"Please don't make me repeat that, Lyssa."

I don't know what to do. I want to punch him for hurting me. But I don't want him to leave. And if I strike back he will. I know he will.

What should I do?

CHAPTER ELEVEN

"But—" she begins to protest.

"But what?" I ask her. I will not repeat my request. I will not. But if she's got something to say I'll listen to her.

"Are you going to hurt me?"

"Do you trust me?"

She shakes her head. Then sucks in a breath, expecting me to react to that.

"That's fine," I say. "I didn't earn it yet. So that's fine. But I told you. I'm on your side."

She exhales. "So…"

"Do you remember what I just asked you to do?"

"Yes," she mumbles.

"Good. Then do it." She looks at my hands. Then back up to my eyes. "Or don't. But I've already told you what happens if you make this hard for me. I'm on your side, Lyssa. I promise."

She kneels on the couch, turns her body, then lies over my legs and buries her face into the cushion.

I lift up her dress, exposing the welts on her ass, and then drag my fingertips over the back of her thigh. Just like I did last night.

She sighs, but her body is still, and rigid, and untrusting.

When I get to the little dent on her knee, I twirl little circles there. Then drag my fingertips all the way down her calf and tickle the sole of her foot.

That's how I wanted to do it last night, but couldn't.

"Does it feel good?" I ask.

"Mmm-hmmm," she mumbles.

"Yeah, I like doing this too. So just relax, Lyssa. Your slate is clean now. We're starting fresh. No more spankings unless you disobey me again."

She's still stiff. Unable to believe me.

That's not a good sign. I wouldn't call myself a dom or anything. I'm not really into this BDSM shit. I know just enough to have fun every once in a while. I've never actually tried to train someone to submit. It was always just a quick game. Little bondage, little spanking, then I come and forget about it.

But that's not what this is now.

I could probably fuck her up worse than she is if I make the wrong move. But if I'm careful with her, if I'm fair with her, if I can earn her trust and then not blow it by going back on my word… well, I think we'll be OK.

I don't really know what her stepfather expects me to do. When we were in the office just before he left I questioned him about that directive to break her.

Break her.

I don't want to break her.

He stammered and stuttered and then changed the wording to tame her. Calm her down. Make her sensible. But he still *meant* break her.

Break her of this wild thing living inside her mind. Make her want to be married.

So OK. I take that to mean he wants her to be polite. And respectful to others. And realize her self-worth. Which, come on, wasn't that his job? Didn't he teach her those things? He's her fucking stepfather.

What he really wants me to do is *parent* her.

Which is weird because I'm doing it with sex. She's motivated by it. That's really all I know about her. If I knew what else motivated her, I'd try that.

Maybe.

I stop playing tickle with her feet and drag my fingers back up to her thigh. She clenches her ass cheeks together when I do that. Which tells me she likes it and it's probably turning her on.

It's wrong. I know that. I don't really have a name for what I'm doing, I just know it's wrong. I might just be some dumb bounty hunter. Some guy who takes jobs that involve kidnapping rebellious corporate princesses. But it's almost an honest living. My mother taught me right from wrong. I don't kill people, for fuck's sake. Up until this job, everyone I've hunted down was a criminal who jumped bail.

Legitimate, all of them

But this one… isn't. She's not a kid, for one thing. Her stepfather has no real right to make her endure this. But I have to do what I have to do to give my mother another chance at life.

I trace one of the bright-red welts on her ass. This makes her hiss in pain. But I don't do anything other than that. Just trace the outline so that *she* knows *I* know what I did to her.

My other hand drops to her hair and I pull it away from her face so I can see her cheek. I really did mean it when I said she didn't need makeup. She's very young and very pretty. She opens one eye to look at me and I smile at her.

She doesn't smile back.

"You OK?" I ask.

She shakes her head no.

"You wanna talk about it?"

She shakes her head no again.

"Do you want me to make you feel better?"

She bites her lip and then nods yes.

My fingers trace a line between her legs and then push their way past the skin of her pressed-together thighs until I find her pussy.

She's not wet so I go slow.

"Like that?" I ask her. "Because you can tell me no if you don't want me to."

She nods yes, then closes her eyes.

I continue playing with her. Pushing one finger in and out of her pussy until she begins to get wet.

One deep breath in, then out, and her body relaxes a little.

Something is wrong with this girl. I just can't put my finger on what it is.

I've had my share of wild ones. And they are all a little fucked up. So that's not so unusual. But she's… damaged. Maybe badly damaged. The way her voice shook when she told me not to hit her with the belt. That was real fear.

It bothers me because she's gone to a lot of trouble to cultivate this wild thing persona. She likes it. She likes being unpredictable and tough. But it's an act, isn't it?

"Should I make you come, Lyssa?" I ask.

Because I now know she uses sex to deflect. And she's faced enough truth today to earn her default defense mechanism.

"Yes," she mumbles.

"OK," I say. But I just continue what I'm doing. Slowly pushing my finger in and out. She earned it. She earned a nice, long, quiet morning of undivided attention.

When she's so wet my finger slides in and out with ease, I drag that wetness down her leg again. Stopping to make little designs in the dent behind her knee.

Then I place all my fingertips on the back of her leg and brush back and forth, back and forth, softly across her upper thigh.

She wiggles a little and I smile.

"Got something to say?" I ask.

"More," she mumbles.

I could make her tell me more what, but that would defeat the purpose of what I'm trying to do. Which is relax her. And reward her too. She didn't want those spankings. No one really wants to be hit with a belt. She just knew that if she wanted me to stay, she had to pay for her disobedience.

So she chose me, didn't she? Over herself.

Her stepfather was wrong. She's not selfish. At least she wasn't in this instance. Selfish means self-preservation. Choosing me was something different.

Choosing me meant opening herself up to something new. Something she was probably afraid of. But she did it.

"I'm proud of you," I say.

"Why?" she mumbles. "Because I gave in?"

"Did you give in?"

"What do you think?"

"I'm not asking what I think. I'm asking what you think."

"A little," she admits.

"Do you know why you did that?" I ask.

"Why?" she says, lifting head up a little to see me.

"No, I'm asking you. Why did you do that? Why did you give in?"

She lowers her head and stays quiet for a few seconds. Then says, "Because I wanted you to stay."

"You don't even know me."

She shrugs. "I like you."

"Why?"

She sighs. Loudly. "Because you… you tell the truth."

"It's not that hard," I say.

"For most people it is."

"Maybe," I admit. "Do you think I'll hit you again?"

She opens her eyes. Thinks about this as she looks at me. "Yes. If I don't do as I'm told, you will."

I nod. "So if I do spank you again, it's because you wanted me to. Understand?"

She nods and closes her eyes again.

"Wild Thing," I say, then chuckle a little. "I think I like you."

And then she smiles.

I do like her. She's kinda easy to like today. Last night, not so much. She did knee me in the balls, punch me in the face—twice—and make me chase her.

Which was kinda fun.

But I don't want to chase her. I don't want her to chase me, either. I don't want to threaten to leave in order to get her to comply. That's not how you build trust.

"Can you turn over?" I ask her. She opens her eyes to look at me. "Or does it hurt too much?"

She thinks about this for a moment. I know it hurts too much. She will not be able to sit today. But I want to see what she decides.

She nods. Then props herself up and I help her turn over and position her ass so it's hanging off the edge of my legs and not pressing too hard against the couch.

"When we're done here I'll go see if there's any ointment I can rub on those welts."

She makes a face at me.

"What?" I ask.

"Nothing," she says.

"I don't want to hurt you, Lyssa. I don't get off on hurting people. So if that's been your experience in the past, forget about it when you're with me. I did it because it was expected. And you were being belligerent."

She sighs.

"But forget about that now," I say, sliding my fingers right between her legs. She's very wet and ready for what I promised her. "Just relax and let me make you feel good."

When I push a single finger inside her she opens her legs a little, granting me permission and access at the same time.

"I want you to fu—" But she stops herself, just in time.

So proud of her.

"You want what?" I ask.

"I want you inside me," she says.

"I am inside you," I say, pumping her with my finger.

"Not like that."

"Then like what?"

She sighs. "I want your… penis inside me."

I laugh, I can't help it.

"What?" She laughs too. "I wasn't sure I was allowed to say c-o-c-k."

"Wild Thing," I say. "I definitely like you."

"Anyway…" She sighs.

"You were saying? You wanted my penis inside you?"

"Yes. I'm very turned on right now."

"Good. You're supposed to be. And don't worry, I'm gonna make sure you come."

"But—"

"Shhhh," I say, placing a fingertip over her lips. "Just enjoy it."

She sighs again. Only this time she relaxes even more. The weight of her body falls into me. I play with her breasts a little, appreciating their fullness, their roundness, and her large, pink nipples.

I lean down and take one in my mouth as I slide a second finger up inside her.

She moans, one hand going to my head and grabbing my hair.

I like that. And the truth is, I want to fuck her. I'm so hard right now. Maybe more turned on than she is. But I can't. Not yet.

I let go of her nipple and straighten up again. Sliding yet another finger inside her. She moans at that. Three fingers is her sweet spot, I realize. Take notes for next time. I'll start with three.

"You know what?" I say.

"What?" she mumbles, moving her hips a little, helping my fingers fuck her better.

"If you're very good I'll let you suck my cock after I'm done with you."

"Will you?" She laughs.

"Yes. Sucking my cock is a gift, Lyssa. I hope you appreciate that. But if you don't want to, then that's cool too."

"I want to," she says. "I do."

"Perfect. Then we both get what we want, don't we? Isn't that kinda nice how it works out that way when you're a good girl?"

"Mmm-hmmm," she says, grimacing when I push all three fingers deep inside her and wiggle them.

I want to make her squirt like she did last night. But I don't want to be rough with her and doing it like this would require me being rough. There's another way, though. One I can try out when I do finally fuck her.

Tomorrow maybe. Or the next day. Or hell, maybe I'll wait until the last day and use that as her reward.

Her hips start moving with the motion of my fingers and I know she's getting close. Her mouth is open now, breathing heavier and faster. Ragged and not at all rhythmic.

I grab her breast and squeeze it hard. Kneading it with my whole palm until she starts to moan. My fingers pressing up inside her as my thumb begins to play with her clit.

"Oh, God," she moans.

Yeah, that's it. Come for me.

I want to flip her around, spread her legs open, and tease her clit with my tongue as she comes on my fingers.

But I can't. She's too sore to be that rough.

So I lean down and kiss her mouth instead. I whisper, "Do you want to suck my cock right now, Lyssa?"

"Mmmm," she moans back as we kiss.

I stop playing with her breast and slide a finger up to her lips. She opens her mouth immediately, wrapping her lips around it.

"Show me," I whisper. "Show me how you'll suck my cock."

She starts bobbing her head up and down, and oh, man. I want to fucking come right now too.

I slip all my fingers out of her pussy, wet and glistening, then place them up to her lips as I take the other one away. She licks them. Hungrily. Eagerly. I take them away and she moans out a protest. But when I slip all four fingers into her pussy and press my thumb up against her clit, flicking back and forth across her sweet spot, she forgets about where they were and only cares about where they are now.

Her mouth opens wide, and her back bucks, and when I begin to pump my fingers inside her as my thumb continues to massage her clit, she lets out a long, slow moan as she comes.

I don't even give her a second to enjoy it, I just sit her up and turn her around with one hand as the other unbuttons and unzips my pants. I pull my cock out and then aim her mouth over my tip.

She sucks me off as I finger her ass. Her head bobbing up and down furiously. Her lips sealed up tight against my shaft. Her tongue flat and wide, pressing along the whole length of me as she takes me deep, then pulls back.

I fist her hair, force her down until her face is pressed up against my stomach, and come in her throat with a long, low, growly moan.

Jesus fucking Christ.

Never in my life has a blow job ever felt so good.

She pulls away, spitting out semen as she sits up.

I smile at her, pet her disheveled mess of blonde hair, and then kiss her on the lips.

"Oh, my God," she whispers into the kiss.

But I just kiss her harder. Wrapping that delicious, unruly mess of hair up in my fist.

She climbs in my lap, hips slightly elevated because of her welts.

And it would be so easy—so fucking easy—to just let her sink down on my cock.

But I don't let her do that.

Not yet, Mason. Not yet.

I control myself and push my cock out of the way, opening my legs wide enough so she can rest the inside of her thighs against mine and relax, and not have to worry about rubbing her welts against my jeans.

She places her head on my shoulder and I wrap my arms around her waist.

Just hold her tight.

Wild Thing, I think in my head. *You're gonna make me love you if you keep acting like this.*

And that's a very bad idea.

I sigh, because that's just the truth.

This girl and me? We have no future together. This was just one of her lessons and nothing more.

Still, I let her cling to me. I let myself cling to her.

And then I go one step further. I hold her tight, lean over, giving her time to reposition her legs, then lie back and pull her on top of me.

She relaxes even more. I didn't think it was possible, but there you have it.

I hold her like that. Her head on my chest. My head pressed against the couch cushions. And I don't ever remember being so relaxed myself.

Her breathing evens out before mine does, letting me know I won. She's relaxed, and calm, and satisfied too.

This is such a mistake. I know better. I might not be very experienced in this whole wild-thing-taming profession, but I know better. Damaged people are easy to hurt. You just give them attention. Show them kindness. Be understanding.

That's all they want. That's all they crave.

And it's wrong. I know it's wrong.

I just don't care at the moment.

I close my eyes and fall asleep with her.

Dreaming about what my life would look like with Lyssa Baylor in it.

CHAPTER TWLEVE

When I wake up I'm alone on the couch. There's a blanket over me and I'm warm.

"Lyssa," Mason says.

I realize he said my name a few times and that's what woke me.

"Hmmm?" I mumble.

"I found some ointment."

"Mmmm," I grumble, too tired and too relaxed to move.

He pulls the blanket off me, takes a seat on the couch, and begins to rub the welt.

"Ow!" I say.

"Sorry."

"You should be. You left marks."

"We already talked about this," he says. "Should we talk about it again?"

"No," I mumble. "I don't want to talk." Mostly because the ointment feels kinda good. And his hand, and his attention, and the way he's careful… all of that feels good too.

"We're not gonna make it to the mall today."

"No?" I ask. "But you don't have clothes."

"I can make do. I was looking forward to grabbing some food. I'm fucking hungry. But then I realized your stepfather said the kitchen was stocked. And I have another lesson to teach you."

"What lesson?" I ask, turning my head so I can look at him. Jesus Christ. He's so fucking handsome, I never want to look away. He's not as put together as he was last night in the club. Shirt untucked, a few unbuttoned buttons so his chest is partly visible. Lips that beg to be kissed and eyes that transfix. This man. How is it that he ended up here with me? What does he do, really? Is this just another typical job for him? Does he tame other girls for money? I have so many questions.

"Cooking," he says. "Do you cook?"

"What?" I say, annoyed that he's thinking about food when I'm thinking about him.

"Good wives cook, Lyssa. So you're gonna make me dinner tonight."

"Are you fuc—" I stop and take a deep breath. "Are you serious?"

"Very," he says. "You must be able to make *something*, right?"

"Ummm… no. I've always had a live-in chef."

"No, you didn't."

"Yes. I did."

"At your apartment right now. Wherever you're living. You have a live-in chef?"

"Yeah," I lie. But only a little lie. I have had a personal chef most of my life. I'm just tired of admitting I'm wrong here. I'm not wrong. I'm right about everything and no one cares. So why not lie about something stupid? Why not make him squirm and deal the way I have to?

"Oh, well." He shakes his head. "That's gotta stop."

"Why? Believe me, Dickerson the Third won't be asking me to cook."

"Doesn't matter. Cooking is something you'll learn before the wedding. So what would you like to cook?"

Before the wedding. Ugh. God, I want to barf. I hold up a finger and say, "Just so we're clear, I'm not marrying that man. I'll hang out here with you until the wedding planners show up, but after that I'm done."

"Lyssa."

"Mason?"

"You have to be here for the wedding."

"No, I don't. And I won't be. Believe me. If I really wanted to leave right now, I could find a way."

He rubs the side of his finger across his forehead and sighs. "How is it that you're engaged to this man?"

"I'm not, I told you that. I never said yes. Do you see a ring on my finger? My stepfather is making this all up."

"Why do you think he's doing that?"

"Why?" I ask.

"Yes, why?"

"I mean, there's a million reasons," I say.

"So give me one."

"Well, he hates that I'm a free spirit."

"Is that what you call it? Because everybody else is calling it Wild Thing."

"It's kind of a cool name though, right? Makes you sing that song in your head, doesn't it?"

He smiles at me. "Explain why he hates that you're a free spirit."

"He wants me to shut my little mouth and do what he says. This isn't rocket science."

"He seems to care about you."

"You *would* think that," I say. "My stepfather is a complete jerk. And my mother was going to divorce him before she died. They had lawyers and everything. So if she had done that before she died, I wouldn't be forced to bend to his will."

"How so?"

"He took my money, Mason. He made me use my trust fund for college."

"Poor you," he says.

Which just pisses me off. Because everyone says that. "Poor Lyssa had to pay her own way through college," I moan. "Yeah, I get it. Sounds ridiculous and doesn't garner much sympathy, but five years of private college pretty much ate up that trust fund. It wasn't *meant* to be used for college. There was other money for college but he stole it from me. That was my security blanket money and now it's all gone. He stole from me then he stopped giving me anything when I moved into my apartment. Oh, he sends money still. But I know what that money is. I don't spend it on me. I do other things with it. Things he would *hate*," I spit.

"Things like drugs, and drinking, and clubbing?"

"Why does everyone assume that?"

"Maybe because that's the image you're presenting?"

"Well, you know what? Other people's presumptions aren't my problem."

"You're trying to make me feel sorry for you, Lyssa. And it's pretty hard to sympathize with your situation. Why don't you just get a job? Isn't that what most college graduates do? And why didn't you just go to a cheaper school? And why did it take you five years to graduate in the first place?"

This is why I don't talk about myself to people. This is why I can't form close bonds with friends. These are the questions they ask me. And you know what? It would take a whole lifetime to explain why all this shit matters and why I'm so pissed off about it.

I'm fucked up. That's the short answer to all those questions. But I'm not going to tell him that. I'm not going to tell anyone that. They can never get past my privilege. They refuse to believe that money, and a country estate, and a well-bred husband won't make all the bad shit disappear

And I stayed in college for five years because I knew what was coming afterward. Marriage. *Forced* marriage. I knew my mother—the only person who ever loved me—was going to leave this world very soon and then

I'd be all alone. And maybe—just maybe… once she was gone he'd leave me alone.

College felt normal and safe. It made me stronger. And when she died shortly before I graduated I felt ready to break free of my insane stepfather for the first time in my life.

She left me an apartment. So I moved in. Money too. But he stole that because it was in a trust he controlled.

He took it all away. And then he sent me checks every month. Anonymous checks, but come on. I knew who they were from. And I knew the price I'd have to pay if I used that money.

Still, I cashed them, didn't I?

And then I spent them on something that would make my stepfather burst with rage if he ever found out.

So I do have a job. That's my job. Cash those checks and use them to show my rage and hate.

But Mason would never believe any of this. He says he's on my side, but he's not. He's on Mason Macintyre's side, not mine. He thinks I'm this wild thing. He thinks I do these things to rebel because I'm spoiled and unappreciative.

So fuck it. I just don't say anything to anyone anymore. And trying to explain myself to Mason was a mistake.

"Are you going to answer me?" he asks.

"No," I say. "I'm not. Because you don't know me and so you can't understand me."

"I'm trying to understand you," he says.

"Well, you're doing a shitty job." He raises an eyebrow at me. But before he can complain about my cussing I say, "Try spanking me with that belt again, Mason Macintyre, and I'll hit you back."

He rubs his jaw, moving it back and forth, then says, "I guess we're even now."

"Hmmm," I grumble.

"You didn't answer my other question."

"What other question?"

"What do you know how to cook?"

"I don't wanna cook," I snap. "I don't want to do any of this shit. And I certainly don't want to get married."

He sighs, then stands up. "Then go to your room."

"Go to my *room*?" I laugh. "What are you? My stand-in father?"

"Well, you're certainly acting like a stand-in teenage daughter."

I fume at that. But I have practiced fuming privately for a very long time so I hold it in. He doesn't deserve to see my anger. He doesn't deserve to *know* me.

I get up, straighten out my wrinkled dress, and say, "Fine."

And then I walk over to the stairs and go up.

I'm just about to turn down the hall to find a new bedroom to occupy when he says, "No. If you want to act like a child, I'll treat you like a child. Go mope in that princess room."

The anger I feel flushes my face with prickling heat. But I don't even look over my shoulder at him. I don't even put up a fight. I've done this routine enough that I know the easiest way out is to go along.

I know what's waiting for me in that room. I know what's coming. And if I'm locked in here for ten days then I'll just have to play the game better than he does, that's all.

But once those ten days are up I'm gone. I will find a way. I will not get lost in the past. I'm *strong* now. I'm *different* now. I'm *better* now.

So I walk down the hallway to the double doors, go upstairs, and flop down in the bean bag chair.

I hate this room. So much. My stepfather put all this crap furniture in here to piss me off. But… maybe… I walk over to the desk and open the top drawer. Oh, yeah. There's one of my old journals. I flip through the pages, but it's empty. I always had a journal when I was a kid. Mostly because my father hated that I kept all my secrets in there. He threw them out every time he found one.

But he must not've checked this desk. It has been over seven years since I used it.

There's more stuff in there. Stuff I'd forgotten about. But it all feels very familiar.

And pretty soon I'm sitting on the beanbag writing.

I write about Mason. Not the kidnapping. I would never place him in the middle of this shit-show of a life I'm leading by outing him in a diary.

I write about what he looks like. And I imagine what it would be like to know him outside of this house.

I bet he'd be nice. I bet he's not a bad guy. He was pretty fair with me all things considering.

I mean… normal me knows that's all wrong.

But princess room me… she has a very warped view of what's normal.

And he sure did make me feel good.

But so what? Maybe he does feel good. Maybe I do enjoy the way his fingers feel inside me.

But none of that matters anymore because he's just another liar.

He's *not* on my side.

No one is on my side.

CHAPTER THIRTEEN

She spends the next five days pouting like a child in that room. Never coming out once. I take her food three times a day and ask her if she's ready to come downstairs.

And each time she says, "No, thank you, Mason."

I have looked through the whole house by now. There is a room in the middle of the hallway that has clothes I presume to be hers.

Jeans and shorts. Shirts and t-shirts. Cotton dresses in pink, and pale yellow, and light blue. There's also underwear. Just plain cotton panties and bras.

Each day I choose something for her to wear and take it up with her breakfast. She offers up no opinions on my selection but she puts them on.

These things make her look younger than she is. I know she's twenty-five, but the day I choose a pair of cut-off shorts, a baseball tee, and a pair of white knee-high socks I have to do a double-take at lunch time because she seriously looks twelve.

She's sitting in the bean bag chair writing in a pink journal with a unicorn on the front. Her pencil has some fuzzy pink topper thing on it. All stuff she found in the little white desk, I suppose.

Turns out, making her learn to cook wouldn't have been a good idea. The kitchen is stocked, but it's very basic stuff and there was a meal plan for her in the pantry. Her stepfather called me that first night to see how she was doing and I asked him about that. He said her food must be controlled to keep her moods stable and I was to follow it precisely.

Oatmeal for breakfast. Grilled cheese and tomato soup for lunch. And either spaghetti with meatballs or hamburgers for dinner.

When I asked him how that crap could possibly even out her moods, he said she liked comfort food. It made her happy and he would like her to be happy.

And even though she doesn't look anything close to happy whenever I go up to her room, she does eat the food.

So I don't argue. Just do as I'm told. Because Baylor did keep up his end of the deal. He wire-transferred that fifty grand directly to my mother and five million dollars appeared in my Swiss bank account. Paid in full. Up front.

And my mother was chosen for that experimental program. I've talked to her a few times over the last several days, but she refuses to answer any questions about the treatment. Just says, "We're going to remain hopeful and positive," and leaves it at that.

I wasn't going to rummage through the office because that seemed like crossing a line. So I didn't. I made it all the way to day five and then… I don't know. I just got bored, I guess.

The office is very grand. Built-in bookshelves line three walls, but the fourth wall has built-in drawers below the windows. They were all locked but I found the keys in the desk.

I feel like staying here in this house, with this girl, has suddenly turned me into someone I'm not. Because Mason Macintyre isn't normally the kind of guy who snoops through people's private papers.

Until yesterday, apparently.

Because I looked through every single drawer. Most of it was boring shit. The deed to the house. Lyssa's name on it. Which I find interesting for a few reasons.

One. If her stepfather is so disappointed with her, then why give her this estate? It's kind of a big-deal place. All the acreage outside, the forest, the lawn, the twenty-one bedrooms. Like… OK. I guess he wants her to start a family. I get that part. But twenty-one bedrooms? Who the hell needs that many rooms? Does he think she's going to open up an orphanage or something? Do they have some huge family that will come visit regularly? I mean, how many kids can one girl push out?

I dunno what she studied in college. I assumed it was something worthless like literature, or history, or art. Or something even more pointless like philosophy. Because the way she talked about her college let me know that it was one of those exclusive private liberal arts colleges. The place you send your daughter to get just enough educated brainwashing for her future career as a politician's wife.

But maybe that private college taught her how to be an event planner? Because this place is more like a hotel than a home. In fact, it's not a home. No one lives in a house like this. No one normal, that is. How would you even keep an eye on those kids? Like… they could get lost in here. It's just so stupid.

The second reason having her name on the deed is the dumbest thing ever is because it's so damn clear she didn't want the estate. So my guess is—first thing this wild girl does when this whole wedding bullshit is over is sell it and get all the money. Then she won't need her stepfather's paycheck anymore.

Didn't he consider this? Or is he so powerful that he's not worried about it? Hell, I imagine it's hard to sell a mansion like this under the best circumstances. And Baylor probably has every real estate agent within three hundred miles in his pocket. Or maybe everyone who could afford it would be too afraid of him to actually go through with the purchase?

I don't know. It makes no sense at all. Fathers who have been perpetually disappointed in their crazy daughters don't go out and buy them a country estate. They just don't.

But then I noticed the date on the deed. It's seven years old.

Seven years? What the fuck? He bought this place for her back when she was eighteen?

Why?

Has been empty this whole time? Lyssa didn't seem familiar with it.

But she was familiar with the furniture in her princess room

What the fuck is going on?

I don't know. But that was just the one drawer. The drawer next to it was even more confusing. It was filled with file folders. And inside the file folders were court papers for Lyssa.

Confusing thing number one about this drawer. She has been arrested sixteen times.

Sixteen. Fucking. Times.

She's only twenty-five, for fuck's sake. How does a girl like her get arrested sixteen times? And they've all happened in the past three years. Probably started around the time she finally managed to get through year five at that stupid over-priced college.

All her court folders are in chronological order and they start off with pretty typical stuff. Public drunkenness. Indecent exposure—I have to stop here and shake my head when I read the full report of how she flashed a cop by opening her legs getting into a limo. Because this would be the moment I'd pull my wild-thing daughter aside and say, "Hey, look, princess. I get that you dig the whole commando thing, but it's time to put some panties on, OK?"

Apparently, Baylor didn't do that. Because the next folder is also indecent exposure with the added bonus of a drug charge.

There's a few more drug charges. Nothing about this is surprising if you've ever seen Lyssa in action. She looks like she does drugs.

Well, at least she did that night I kidnapped her. That heavy makeup on her eyes. All darked up and smoky. Her glossy lips and contoured cheekbones. The long, wild mane of blonde hair that gives off a just-fucked vibe, and that gold dress.

A predator. She looked like a predator that night.

And all her mugshots are sexy as fuck. I'm talking… why the hell all the tabloids haven't run these yet is beyond me. These mugshots could be on the cover of every grocery-store magazine.

It's so wrong to be thinking that. Because if these pictures were on the cover of magazines they'd also be in every man's bathroom.

And thinking about guys jerking off to her face just pisses me off.

She doesn't look like her mugshots so much anymore. She looks like a damn teenager now. And not the wild kind, either. She looks like… you know. Typical Daddy's girl princess.

OK. So the charges all pretty much make sense until I get up to number ten. Then things get weird.

Because she gets arrested for prostitution.

Just… what?

Lyssa? Prostitution?

I can't see it. I mean, I've seen her in action. Hell, I've been on the receiving end of her animal instincts. But selling her body for money?

Then again, she did tell me she was broke. Maybe she did?

There's two of those, then shit really goes off the rails. Because the last few weren't for prostitution, they were for pimping and pandering.

What the *what?*

I literally had to read that four times to make it sink in.

Lyssa Baylor is a *madam?*

Get the fuck out of here.

But there it was. All in black and white. Her sexy-as-fuck face front and center in each of those mugshots.

And she was found guilty too.

I shuffled through every file and realized she was found guilty every single time. And each time, her stepfather got her off with community service and a steep fine. Some of the more recent fines were in the millions.

Must be nice to be rich. That fucker bought judges.

But I thought about that all damn afternoon as I cooked comfort food for Lyssa as she sat up in her princess tower and scribbled away in her journal.

If he could buy off her sentences… why didn't he just buy off her crimes?

Why leave her with this long record?

So I went through it all again and at the end of every single file was a single piece of paper, signed by the same judge, which had a big red stamp on it that said RESTRICTED DISCLOSURE.

I didn't even know what that meant. I had to look it up and apparently people can like… hide criminal records from the public using this restricted disclosure thing.

Then I got lost on the internet looking up legal terms. Like what is the difference between a sealed file and a restricted disclosure file?

Because it's all kinda weird.

If Baylor has the power to buy off a judge at the sentencing stage and get her entire criminal history marked with this restricted disclosure thing, why not just do it from the start and get her off with charges dismissed?

Was he trying to teach her a lesson?

Maybe.

God, the guy is kind of a dick.

Not that she's an innocent victim here. Jesus Christ. Her rap sheet is worse than a lot of the scumbags I know in the bounty-hunting business.

But… I don't know. I'd want to protect my daughter from all this. I'd definitely have done something drastic before it got to this point.

Or at least, I tell myself that.

Maybe that's why her stepfather is doing this to her now? This is an intervention. Not a typical one, from what I understand of interventions. But rich people. They're not typical.

On the morning of day six I'm sick of oatmeal, I'm sick of grilled cheese, and if I have to make another meatball I might lose my mind. Plus, I only have four days to get her ready for the wedding planners and her stepfather, and she hasn't even tried on the dress yet.

So that's my plan for today. Enough moping. She's coming out of that room.

I open the double doors and yell, "Come down here, Lyssa."

She huffs back at me from above.

"Now," I say.

When she appears at the top of the stairs she's wearing a new combination of clothes. Things I brought to her over the past several days, but not an outfit I chose.

Red athletic shorts that are so short and tight, if she were to turn around I'm pretty sure her ass cheeks would be hanging out. I brought those up the other day but she didn't put them on. Just lounged around in her underwear that day. Teasing me and tempting me by opening her legs each time I brought her food.

Her top is a stretchy white t-shirt that hugs her curves and I can tell, even from down here, that she has no bra on because her nipples are hard. She didn't wear that the day I brought it up either, opting instead to wear a pink zip-up hoodie with nothing underneath, the zipper down far enough that I caught a glimpse of her tits when she made a point to bend over and pick something up off the floor.

And extra-long, thigh-high tube socks. Which I brought the first night as part of her sleepwear ensemble. Apparently she doesn't sleep naked. Because she put this stuff on without comment. All the pajamas were long nightshirts with cartoon characters on them.

Right now she's staring at me from the top of the stairs, snapping her gum, and her long, blonde hair has been pulled up into two pigtails that are each curled into a loose spiral.

No wonder her stepfather treats her like a child. She certainly dresses, eats, and acts like one. Because right now, this image of her in this moment, was all *her choice*.

"What?" she snarls, bratty teenage princess on full display.

"You need to try on your wedding dress," I say.

She huffs, but begins to descend the stairs. I step aside to let her pass and get a whiff of perfume. Something overly sweet. Like baby powder.

"Which room?" she asks, swinging her hips as she walks down the hall. I catch a glimpse of her ass cheeks, because yes. They are hanging out. There's the tell-tale remnants of a yellow-green bruise from where I smacked her with the belt that first day across the bottom where her ass meets her thigh.

"The one with the open door," I reply.

She saunters in, still enticing me with her hips, and I follow her.

The dress is hanging on the back of the open closet door, sealed up in a white bag.

"Take it out and put it on," I say. "The seamstress needs to know if it fits."

She pulls the zipper down on the bag, takes the dress out, and lays it across the bed.

"It's pretty," I say, trying to be helpful and break her out of this mood. I'm sick of it. Really had enough. Her wedding day can't come fast enough if you ask me. I think back on that first day we spent here and how I thought I liked her, but it had to have been the sex. Or the spankings. Or something. Because right now she's nothing but high-maintenance and tiresome. And that criminal record. I should not have snooped. I liked her a lot more before I learned she was this drugged-up exhibitionist who likes to sell herself and other women.

"Pretty?" she says, lifting one eyebrow at me. "I guess. If you like cascading organza ruffles in pink and a sweetheart neckline. Who the hell wears pink on their wedding day, anyway?"

Yeah, she's got a point there. It's fugly. Fugly as fuck. Like Cinderella's fairy godmother threw up a ruffled pink pumpkin and this is what came out. "So I take it you didn't choose this dress?" I ask.

"Do you think I chose *this*?" she says, panning her hands down her body to indicate her present outfit.

"Actually, you did. I didn't bring that ensemble to you."

"Right." She snorts. Then lifts her shirt over her head and throws it on the floor.

I know I should turn away, but she instantly goes from bratty teenager to seductive grown-up. And her tits are just as beautiful as I remember. So I look at them.

She places one foot on the bed, right on top of the wedding dress, and begins rolling down her thigh-high knee sock.

I watch, unapologetically, as she repeats that process with the other leg.

Then she turns to face me, smiles, and twirls around as she slides her shorty-shorts over her hips, wiggling her ass like a stripper doing a tease.

"Lyssa," I say.

She kicks the shorts off one foot without comment and reaches for the dress. Unzipping the back and stepping into it. Once it's on she walks over to me and says, "Zip me, please," then lifts her pigtails up, even though they're not in the way of the zipper. She did that so I'd notice how her breasts rise up.

"Turn around," I say, twirling my finger.

She does, and even though I'm trying my best not to touch her bare skin—because I am totally hard right now and I don't need any more encouragement. I'm not going to mess with this girl again. Not gonna do it—my fingertips brush along her back when I reach for the zipper and my cock jumps a little.

She sucks in a breath and part of me knows she did that so I could zip her up, but some other part of me wishes it was because of my touch.

When the zipper's up she drops her pigtails and lowers her arms. Turns to look in the mirror on the back of the closet door, and our eyes meet in the reflection.

"It's gross," she says, smoothing down the huge ruffles of her long skirt.

"It's nice," I say. And it is. I mean, OK. The dress is fugly, but on her it actually looks good.

"Yeah, if this were my sweet sixteen and I had no taste. Sure, I guess."

I laugh. I can't help it. "So tell him to get you a different dress."

She rolls her eyes in the mirror. "I don't even care."

"Look," I say, reaching for one of her pigtails to pull the elastic off. I do that again with the other one, then arrange her hair so her long, loose curls fall over her shoulders. "That's better, right?"

She studies herself. Turning a little to the left, then to the right. Picking up her layered skirt with her fingertips, then letting go. "Little bit."

"Well… I was planning on making you go to the mall with me today. I know you like comfort food and everything, but I can't eat any more of that shit. I was hoping you'd be agreeable and we could go out. So maybe we shop for another dress? I have money. I'll pay for it."

She looks at me in the mirror and frowns.

"What?"

"You want to buy me a wedding dress?"

"If you want a new one, I will."

"Hmm," she says.

"So that's a yes?"

She shrugs. "Why not. Unzip me." She lifts her long hair up, because this time she really needs to, and I can't help myself. I watch her breasts rise in the mirror.

I unzip the dress, exposing her bare back again, and then she drops her hair and it brushes against the back of my hands.

My cock is really jumping now.

"Take it off me," she whispers.

"Lyssa," I say, shaking my head.

"Come on," she says, meeting my eyes in the mirror. "Just help me out of the dress, Mason."

There is this internal debate running through my head. On the one hand, she's clearly unstable. Needs a lot of therapy, this one. And she's going to marry some guy in a little over a week. She's trying on her wedding dress, for fuck's sake. So there is no other answer to her request except a very firm no.

And never mind that we've already fooled around, that was before I realized how messed up she is. If we did it now, I'd be taking advantage of her.

But on the other hand… she's not married yet. Plus, that whole we've-already-messed-around argument kinda goes both ways. And she doesn't even want to get married. I'm ninety percent certain it's not gonna happen, even if I do manage to get her to "the day".

"Do you always weigh your choices so carefully?" she asks.

"I try to," I say.

"Then you think too much," she says, reaching for both my hands and placing them on her shoulders.

My fingertips grab the edges of her sleeve caps and drag them down, exposing her bare skin.

Our eyes meet again in the mirror.

"Don't stop now," she says. "You're almost there."

I know better. I should not be doing this. Because there's only one way this ends and that's with her flat on her back on top of that bed.

But I do it anyway. I drag the sleeve caps down her arms until her breasts fall out—and then I stop. My hands slowly falling to the top of her hips.

I look at her in the mirror. She looks nothing like the little brat who came down the stairs. Every bit a woman now.

My hand comes up to cup her breast and she sucks in air, making her ribcage protrude just enough so I notice. I flit my fingers over her ribs on the other side and she shudders as a chill runs through her body, prickling her skin and making her nipples tight and firm.

She reaches for the skirt of her dress, sliding it over her hips until it falls into a puddle of pink ruffles at her feet.

Now she is bare.

I'm shirtless and wearing my same jeans from that first day. Forced to wash them, and my shirt, over and over again since we got here, due to her tantrum. And for a moment I feel a flash of anger over that.

Being trapped here. Blackmailed into doing her stepfather's bidding. All because of *her*.

"You're a brat, you know that? A spoiled-rotten brat."

She stares at me in the mirror.

I slide my hand up to her neck and press my palm flat against her throat. Feel her swallow, then imagine her doing that to my cock.

She swallows again, reading my mind. Enticing me to keep going even when I know damn well I should stop.

Her hand finds mine and a moment later she's leading me over to a chair.

I shake my head at her. "No. We're not gonna do this."

But she drops to her knees and pops the button on my jeans. Drags the zipper down with her teeth, all the while staring me in the eyes.

I remember the insults I lobbed at her that first day. *Slut.* I called her a slut.

And hell, she might be.

But there's always an underlying reason for that, so—

"Just shut up," she says, pulling out my hard cock and squeezing it in her palm.

"What?"

"You're thinking so fucking hard right now I can practically hear the spinning in your mind."

I raise an eyebrow at her.

"I'm over your rules, Mr. Macintyre. *So* over them. I don't care what you do. I don't care what you want, or what you say. I don't even care if you leave as long as you do it after. Because I care about me, OK? *Me.* And this is what I want."

She opens her mouth and places my cock on her tongue.

I should throw her on the bed and spank her silly. Will do that, later. But right now I can't help myself.

Wild thing... I really like you.

I know I shouldn't. I've been complaining about her all week. Insisting she's nothing more than a spoiled little rich girl.

Talking myself into believing that the reason I have to jerk off three times a day isn't because she's in the same house as me.

Isn't because I've been picturing her in my mind. Seeing her that first night. Running away from me.

Isn't because she wears these tantalizing teenage outfits.

Isn't because of the pigtails and thigh-high tube socks.

But it is. It's all of that.

I'm fucking sick. I like her dressed up like a doll. I like feeding her grilled cheese and oatmeal. I like the way she snaps her gum and—

Get your fucking shit together, Macintyre.

"Lyssa," I say, placing a hand on her head. "This isn't right."

But instead of pulling her off me, I push her face into my stomach.

She takes me deep as I say, "This is wrong, on so many levels."

And then I begin moving my hips so I can fuck her mouth and add, "We need to stop."

She opens her throat, letting the tip of my dick hit the back of her soft palate as I grab her hair and begin bobbing her back and forth on my cock.

Saliva runs out over her plump, pink lips. Her eyes begin to water. Her hair is a tangled mess in my hands, and her legs are open so she can play with herself.

I close my eyes and make myself do it.

I pull her off me and hold her there as I try to get these sick urges under control.

Her hands wrap around the back of my thighs, urging me forward again, and I can't help myself. The imagery, the scent of her wet pussy in the air, the throbbing of my cock.

There is no way I can stop now. Not when she's compelling me to continue.

She comes up for air and says, "Sit down."

And I do. The chair is right behind me so it's almost too easy to give in.

I want to fight it. I want to do the right thing and put a stop to this before it goes too far.

Which is a joke. It's already gone too far. But I can try to talk myself into believing that it hasn't...

If I don't actually fuck her.

If I attribute my transgressions back on that first day to the fact that I was weak and blackmailed into being here by her stepfather.

If I put a stop to this right now…

But she's licking the tip of my cock, and pumping me with her hand, and playing with herself between her legs and I get it in my head that if I don't come now— right fucking now—I'll never come again.

So I do.

I lean back, groaning as she pumps my cock hard, jerking me to full climax, and then she aims my tip at her face and I come all over it in long, spurting streams.

CHAPTER FOURTEEN

I grab the wedding dress and use it to wipe his come off my face.

"Lyssa!" Mason yells. "What the fuck?"

"You said you were gonna buy me another one." I blink my eyes at him innocently.

He's standing up in an instant, pulling me to my feet. He bends me over the edge of the bed and his hand comes down hard on my ass.

"Ohhh," I moan. Because it feels good. I've been thinking about his hard slaps all week. Trying to push his buttons. But he's been the model of control. A perfect little babysitter. Giving in and letting me do as I please. And I'm tired of it. I'm tired of getting my way.

I want the punishment.

"You want another one?" he asks, pulling my hair.

I'm about to say, *Yes! I want all the spankings!*

"I was going to buy you another dress to make you happy, Lyssa. Not because you decided to defile the one you were given."

"What?" I say.

"What the fuck is wrong with you?"

"What the fuck is wrong with me? What the fuck is wrong with you?"

"Why did you just rub come all over that dress?"

"Mason," I say, laughing a little. "No one cares about that dress."

"That's your problem, you know. You think everything's free. It was a gift. And fine, you don't like it and every girl deserves the dress of their dreams on their wedding day, so I don't mind giving you that. But you didn't have to fucking ruin it!"

"Are you serious right now?" I struggle to stand up but he holds me in place with a hand pressed hard between my shoulder blades.

"I'm very fucking serious," he growls.

"I just sucked your cock and you're mad at me for ruining a stupid dress?"

"You have no respect for anything, do you?"

"What are you even talking about? We were in the middle of dirty sex and—Oh, I get it."

"Get what?"

"You feel guilty. I should've known. That's a typical man response. You can't control your urges so—"

"My urges? You practically begged me to fuck you!"

"Oh, really?" I say, so snarky. "No. That's not what this is. You want me. You dream about me, don't you? Picturing yourself fucking me. But you don't want to admit you want me. I'm fucked up, right? Disturbed. And you can't soil your own self-righteousness with psycho Lyssa. And you're this high-and-mighty moral asshole who thinks he's too good."

"I think I'm too good?" He laughs. "That's all you!"

I narrow my eyes at him. "Do you want to spank me, or don't you?"

"Yes!" he yells.

"Then do it!"

He smacks me hard and I squeal. Then again, and again, and again and—he stops.

I'm breathing hard, pressing my face into the mattress. My fingers gripping the comforter tightly.

He removes his palm from my back and I scramble all the way on to the bed and turn around to face him.

He's grabbing at his hair, shaking his head.

"What's wrong with you?" I ask.

"I don't know," he says. "I don't know."

He tucks his dick away and sits back down in the chair. Hand over his eyes as he rubs his forehead.

"Mason," I say.

"What?" he mumbles.

"What's going on?"

He looks up at me from under his hair. Shakes his head.

"What?"

"This place is fucked up, that's what."

"Why do you think I didn't want to live here? Jesus Christ." I sigh. Because this shit is not rocket science, yet no one but me seems to be able to figure it out.

What is wrong with people?

"I don't know what I'm doing," he says, hiding his face again. "I have no idea what I'm doing here with you."

"You're… working?" I offer. Because he looks pretty distressed and, try as I might to hate this man, he's just not hateable. He's actually kind of adorable. Nothing like any of the boys or men I've dated in the past.

He moves his hand away from his eyes. "Working?"

I shrug. "Well, you're getting paid."

"To do what?"

"I don't know. Make me… better? I guess. Change me into whatever it is my stepfather told you to?"

He stares at me for a minute. "You wanna know what he told me to do?"

I don't know if I want to know that. I really don't.

But Mason tells me anyway. "He told me to *break you,* Lyssa. What the fuck is he talking about?"

"My bad attitude?" I say, guessing.

He laughs. But I can tell it's an ironic laugh and not a funny-haha laugh.

"I'm sorry," he says.

"For what?"

"For all of this. I think I should just go."

"Go? No, Mason. Please. Don't go."

"Why do you even want me here? You don't know me, so you don't like me. And I've done nothing but harass you and keep you locked up in that stupid bedroom. You should want me to go."

I wilt a little. Because I do like him. And I haven't even been miserable upstairs in that room. Confused and possibly regressing. But I looked forward to him bringing me food and choosing me clothes. I liked making him frustrated and flustered. It's all sorts of fucked up and I can't even begin to explain why I feel this way or why I do these things, I just know one thing. I don't want him to leave.

"I'll be good," I whisper. "If you stay, I'll be good."

CHAPTER FIFTEEN

She'll be good.

"I'll go to the mall with you," she says. "And we can eat something else. Not spaghetti and meatballs or hamburgers."

She'll be good.

"Mason."

"What?"

She sucks in a deep breath and lets it out. "I promise. I'll be good. You can't leave anyway. You got paid already, right?"

I nod, but don't look her. I did get paid. A lot of fucking money. And my mom is in the experimental treatment program. So her stepfather held up his end and not only am I not holding up mine, I feel like I'm making everything worse. I feel like I'm making *her* worse. I just can't put my finger on what's wrong here.

I mean, I know the whole thing is wrong. She's wrong, he's wrong. The estate, the criminal record, the marriage. All of it is so very wrong.

But I don't have a firm grip on *why* it's wrong.

Baylor's excuse for why he wants his daughter to marry this guy makes some sense. In one breath I believe him. He's worried about her. And anyone who spends time with this girl gets that she's disturbed. So is it so bad that he wants to take care of her?

But when I take another breath I see it another way. This place. That room. Those clothes, that food—it gives me a sick feeling inside.

"I'll do whatever you want. I'll… I'll clean the dress. We can take it to the dry cleaners at the mall and—"

"Fuck that dress. It's ugly as sin."

"OK, well… I won't try to seduce you anymore."

I still don't look at her but I do crack a smile.

"Please," she says, scrambling off the bed to kneel at my feet.

Good God. Why does she have to do that?

She rests her head on my knee, wrapping her hands around my leg. "Don't leave me here. I promise to do whatever you say."

"Everything?" I ask, finally meeting her eyes.

She nods. "Yes. Everything."

"You'll stop swearing?"

"Yes."

"And be polite?"

"Yes, I promise."

"And respect yourself and others."

"Um… yeah. Of course. But what exactly do you mean when you say respect myself?"

Is she kidding me right now? "Lyssa," I say.

"What?"

"You know what I mean."

"OK, so… I won't take five years to finish college, or waste money, or wipe my face with my wedding dress, or—"

"That's not what I'm talking about." Jesus. How is she so clueless?

"I don't understand."

"Respect yourself. Don't wear those clothes, or put your hair up in pigtails like you're a little girl, or eat comfort food at every meal. You need to grow up, OK? You need to *grow the fuck up!*"

She stares at me for a moment. Shocked by my outburst. Hell, I'm kinda shocked by my outburst too.

"OK," she finally says.

"You'll do that?"

She nods. "I promise. I will."

I close my eyes and wonder if it's good enough. I feel like I'm losing myself by being around this girl. Like she's twisting me into something I'm not. And I don't like it. I like her… but I don't like how she makes me feel.

It feels dirty.

She makes me feel dirty.

Wild Thing. She sure is.

"Mason," she says.

"What?"

"Just… please. Can we go to the mall?"

We do go to the mall. There are three cars to choose from in the attached five-car garage and she shows me where the keys are. I still have the van, but that van is creepy as all fuck when I look at it. I kidnapped her in that van.

What the hell was I thinking when I took this job?

Well, that's easy. I was thinking about my mother. I needed that fifty grand pretty bad that day. And Baylor was blackmailing me.

Still, both those reasons feel a whole lot like excuses right now.

Why does this girl affect me this way? I don't understand it.

Anyway. We take the brand-new Mercedes to the mall. White with tan leather interior and every gadget you can think of. Is it weird that Lyssa matches her car?

Because Lyssa kept her promise and managed to put together an outfit from her closet in her real bedroom that doesn't show off her tits or her ass.

A shapeless dress that has a high collar and hits her just above the knee. It's white, not pink, and her shoes have a heel on them, so that's a plus. At least she doesn't look like my fucking daughter.

I wear... the same thing I've been wearing. Which only serves to remind me that I didn't plan on being here for ten days. This was an in-and-out job and now it's not.

Or it is, if you have a dirty mind. Which I apparently do. I'm going crazy. This job, this girl, this house—all of it is making me crazy.

When we get to the mall I take Lyssa's hand—I don't know why I do that either. I just do—and we walk around looking at shops.

"Where do we find a wedding dress?" I ask.

"I have no idea," she says. "I haven't been to a mall since I was twelve."

I laugh at that. "Me either."

"Blind leading the blind," she says, leaning into me. "Let's shop for you first."

So we do. Not a department store, which is where I usually get my clothes, but a designer label that has its own boutique. But I'm a quick shopper. I know exactly what I like and soon we're out in the mall walking past the lingerie store.

Lyssa stops.

I shake my head at her.

"This is grown-up," she says. "Those bras and panties you've been giving me are for little girls."

God, it sounds kinda sick when she says it like that.

"Come on," she says, tugging me into the store.

A saleswoman comes over immediately. Smelling money, or desperate for conversation, or hell, maybe she really does just want to make sure Lyssa gets the perfect-fitting bra.

They disappear into a dressing room while I browse the goods, stopping at the nighties. I have never bought underwear for a woman before. Mostly because I always make sure I do not have a girlfriend on Valentine's Day when such a purchase is expected. But I could see Lyssa wearing some of this stuff.

I pick one off the rack, walk over to the dressing room, and hand it to the woman helping her. "Tell her to try this one on."

She waggles her eyebrows at me, and even though I have a desire to put distance between myself and what she's inferring, I keep my mouth shut and don't even try to explain. There's no good way to explain who and what Lyssa is to me in this moment, anyway.

Lyssa giggles in the dressing room. Yells, "Mason, are you out there?"

"I'm right here," I say.

"What's this for?"

"Your wedding night," I say. "Unless you have something already."

"I don't," she says. "But I love it. It's very grown up."

"Good," I say, cringing at her words. The saleslady is waggling again. *Oh, wedding*, that waggle says. I ignore her. Because I do not want to discuss the wedding I'm not a part of.

When Lyssa gets tired of trying things on, she emerges triumphant and hands the saleswoman a whole armful of pretty bras and panties. And the nightie.

"Fits," she says, shrugging one shoulder at me.

I pay for it all, because I did promise her new underwear.

But I like paying for it. Feels good to have a lot of money. I'm not poor, by any means. But that's mostly because I'm a saver by nature. My jobs are here and there. Sometimes I'm super busy, sometimes I'm not. I've learned to live below my means.

When we're done there we head into another boutique that sells dresses and Lyssa chats with the saleswoman about something that might be appropriate for a wedding.

"What do you think I should get, Mason?"

"Up to you," I say.

"No, really," she says. "I want to know your opinion."

This exchange earns us a weird look of confusion from the saleswoman.

"Not pink," I say.

"No." She laughs. "I still want white."

"No ruffles," I say.

"Done," she says.

"How about this one?" I point to a very sophisticated dress on a mannequin. Long, fitted, satin, two slits up the side, crystal beads covering the tight bodice, and strapless.

"I'd like to try that one on," Lyssa tells the woman.

She smiles at me as she turns to follow the woman to the dressing room, and I look around. Wondering how one chooses just the right dress for her wedding day. Then feel guilty for choosing Lyssa's dress for her.

I wander over to the dressing area just as the saleswoman—Margaret, her name tag says—comes out, almost bumping into me.

"Oh," she says. "Sorry."

"Totally my fault," I say.

"You're Mason?" she asks.

"Yes."

"And you're not the fiancé?"

"No," I say.

"Hmmmm."

"What?"

"She wants you with her. She's in room six." And then she gives me a stern look, which I fail to understand.

I wander in, looking for room six, and find the door open. "You beckoned," I say.

"Unzip me," she says. "And close the door."

I close the door, notice that the room is walled in on all four sides for maximum privacy, then walk over and pull her zipper down as she lifts up her hair. My cock suddenly reminds me that I did this very thing a few hours ago and it ended up getting sucked. Cocks remember stuff like that. They are easily trained that way. Get it once, they expect it every time.

I suck in a deep breath as she lowers her dress over her shoulders and lets it fall to the ground.

She's not wearing a cotton bra anymore. And her panties were definitely not made for a little girl.

"I see you wore something home from the last store."

"Do you like it?" she asks, looking at me in the mirror.

And again, my cock is saying… *Are we having a Groundhog Day? Because I could swear we just did this. And if it happened once…*

Easy there, fella. Don't get excited. It's not gonna happen again.

He doesn't listen. Because Lyssa looks like a fucking lingerie model in her matching yellow bra and panty set. All she needs is a pair of those huge wings and she could be on the runway.

"I'll take that as a yes," Lyssa says.

"Knock, knock," a voice says on the other side of the door.

Lyssa goes over to the door, opens it a crack, takes the dress, and says, "No, thank you, we've got it."

Then shuts it in her face.

"Lyssa," I say.

"I said thank you," she protests. "I wasn't being rude."

"Maybe she should help you get the dress on?"

"No."

I cock an eyebrow at her.

"What? I'm not seducing you. I'm standing way over here, see? And besides, you picked it out. Don't you want to see it on?"

Which is dumb. Because I could wait outside and still see it on her when she's finished.

"Put the bags down, Mason. I need your help."

I drop the bags and walk over to her as she unzips the new dress, removes it from the hanger, and says, "Hold it, so I can step in."

"Lyssa," I say.

"Just please," she begs. "You're making a big deal out of nothing."

Which is not true. She's playing games with me again. And my cock is doing its best to play along, against my better judgement.

I hold it, back side facing her, and she puts her hands on my shoulders to steady herself as she steps inside the dress. I pull it up her body and she holds it against her breasts, then turns and says, "Zip me."

I do, and again, I feel like this day is on repeat. Which is making me think about how she sat at my knees and sucked my dick.

When it's zipped she turns to face me. "What do you think?"

I place both hands on her shoulders and turn her to the mirror. "What do you think?"

She smiles at herself in the mirror. "Now *this* is a wedding dress."

And I agree. So different than the one she used to wipe my come off her face.

"But oh," she says, turning to look at her ass in the mirror. "Panty lines."

And then, before I even realize what she's doing, she reaches inside the side slits along each thigh and pulls her panties down, kicking them off to the side.

"Lyssa!"

"This is why I never wear underwear," she explains. "I need to see if it looks OK without them. Because with them—"

"You are not walking down the aisle with no panties on."

"Oh, yes, I am. This is a no-panties dress and you picked it out. So you have to live with it."

My cock agrees with her. Because I'm fully fucking hard now.

She glances down at it, then lifts her eyes to mine, and says, "I hope you're not thinking—"

"I'm not," I say.

"—because if you wanted to do dirty stuff in here, we could get caught—"

"Don't worry," I say.

"—and Margaret would be so disappointed in us if she caught the best man fucking his best friend's fiancée."

"What?" I say, doing a double-take.

"That's what I told her. It's kinda hot, isn't it?"

"No," I say. "It's kinda sad, actually."

"Well, it was a lie, anyway. So that just makes it hot."

"Jesus, Lyssa."

She mouths the words *Wild Thing* at me, then reaches down to grab my cock.

I push her away, but she backs me into the mirror with a bang.

"Everything OK in there?" Margaret calls from the other side of the door.

"Just fine," I yell back, glaring at Lyssa.

"Come on," she whispers. "Wild thing, hold me tight." And then she giggles.

"That's not even how the song goes—"

But I stop. Because the next thing I know, she's on her knees in front of me, the button popped on my jeans, the zipper down, and my cock is in her hands.

"Lyssa," I groan.

"Tell me no," she says, then sticks the head of my cock in her mouth, pressing her tongue up against my shaft, before I even have a chance.

"Would you like another dress?" Margaret calls.

Lyssa eases her mouth off my cock with a loud smacking sound and looks up at me. "What do you think, Mason? Do we need to try on another one?"

"No," I call back to Margaret. "We'll let you know if we need anything else."

"I could wrap it up for you," Margaret offers, just as Lyssa puts my cock back in her mouth and takes me deep into her throat.

"Uh… we're not quite…. oh, God… done yet," I say.

"OK, I'm right out here if you need anything."

"Great," I groan. Because Lyssa is giving me a full-on head-bobbing messy blow-job. And against my better judgment, my fingers are now tangled in her hair, urging her on.

She pulls off me, both her hands on my thighs, pushing me back, and then she stands again.

"What are you doing?" I ask.

"Making you choose."

"Choose what?"

She backs up against the mirror and whispers, "You know why you chose the dress with two slits?"

I already know where this is going.

"Because I can do this." She pulls the center portion of material aside and flashes her bare pussy at me. "And you," she says, grabbing my shirt and pulling me towards her so my cock bumps into her leg, "can put that inside me and I don't even have to take my clothes off."

"I'm not gonna fuck you," I whisper back.

Why not? she silently mouths and simultaneously pouts.

"Because you're not mine, Lyssa."

She sighs. Frowning. Giving up. Because she leans back against the wall and wilts. "I want to be yours."

"You can't be," I say.

"Why not?"

"Because you're engaged. And I'm just… I'm just your fucking babysitter."

She slides her hand between her legs, then withdraws it and places the tip of her glistening wet finger against my lips.

I close my eyes and open my mouth, my cock totally in charge now. I suck on her finger the way she was just sucking on my cock.

"Please," she whispers. So low, I almost don't hear her. "I promise to be good in every other way if you just… make me feel loved right now."

I pull her finger out of my mouth and say, "Lyssa," feeling sad for her.

"We can pretend," she says. "Right?" She places both her hands on my cheeks and leans in. Kisses me.

I kiss her back.

I know I shouldn't. I feel the guilt of a best man fucking his best friend's fiancée, and I don't even care.

If her name is Lyssa Baylor then I *want* to fuck my best friend's fiancée.

"Everybody pretends," she whispers past my lips. "It's all fake, Mason. So who cares, anyway?"

She pulls her dress aside again, reaching for my cock. And when she tugs on it, I do the unthinkable. I take two steps forward and we're not even two steps apart. So now my chest is pressing up against her breasts, forcing her against the wall. She lifts up her leg and I brush the middle section of satin dress over the side of her thigh to get it out of the way.

And after that, it takes no effort at all to slip my cock inside her.

The one thing I told myself I wouldn't do.

I would eat her out, and let her blow me. And kiss her, and suck her nipples, and smack her ass, and all that other stuff. And it would be OK if I just didn't fuck her.

And now I'm fucking her.

In her wedding dress.

Which I picked out.

Which she is wearing for me.

And I will not be the one waiting for her at the end of that aisle when that wedding day finally catches up to her.

"Wild Thing," she whispers past my lips as I kiss her and fuck her slowly.

I think I love her.

Because I can't stop this. Even if I wanted to—and I don't—I can't stop this. And even though I know stupid Margaret probably has her ear up to the door, listening as I slide my cock in and out of Lyssa's wet pussy, I *won't* stop this.

Lyssa hikes her leg up higher and I reach down, pick up her other one, and press her back against the wall as I begin to thrust harder.

She moans, then bites her lips to make herself be quiet.

And I moan, and she places her fingers over my lips to make me be quiet.

And then Margaret is knocking and asking us questions and we ignore her. Just… ignore her. Because Lyssa's breathing heavy, like an animal. And I'm doing the same.

And we are just animals.

We are just… wild things.

CHAPTER SIXTEEN

Margaret can go fuck herself. What does she care if we have hot sex in the dressing room? We bought the stupid dress.

Mason holds my hand all the way back to the car. He's got my bagged-up wedding dress over his shoulder and I'm carrying the rest of the shopping bags.

We look like a power couple who just went crazy with the credit card.

And I love it.

He lays the dress carefully across the back seat of the Mercedes and the rest of the bags go into the trunk.

I'm already sitting in the passenger seat when he gets in his side and starts the car, then glances over at me. Opens his mouth to say something, then closes it again.

He puts the car in gear, then back in park.

"I know what you're going to say," I say, looking at him.

He stares at me, but keeps quiet.

"I broke the deal. I'm sorry, not sorry. And if you want to leave when we get home, or spank me, or beat me with the belt to make me understand that what I did was wrong, then fine. It was worth it."

"That's not what I was gonna say."

"Oh."

He sighs. "I was gonna say… we need rules."

"What kind of rules?"

"Maybe just… an understanding."

"OK."

"You're going to marry that guy next week, Lyssa. And I'm going to Sweden to be with my mom."

"That's our understanding?"

"No," he says, shaking his head. "Well, half of it. That's what's gonna happen in a week. But until then, just… fuck it, ya know."

"Fuck it?" I say, raising my eyebrows.

"Yeah, fuck it."

And then he puts the car back in reverse, backs out, and we drive away from the mall.

But we don't go home. We stop and eat first. He gets a steak and I get a grilled chicken salad, and then we stop at the grocery store and get things that are not oatmeal, or grilled cheese, or spaghetti.

And we talk about what kind of cereal we like, and if we should buy cage-free brown eggs or just the regular white ones. And what we should cook for the next week.

On the way home after that he tells me about his mom, and where he's gonna go in Sweden, and I tell him about the trip my stepfather booked for my honeymoon.

"Alaska?" he says. "I mean, I like Alaska. I'd totally go to Alaska. But on a honeymoon?"

"Dickerson probably wants to kill me and leave my body in the woods for the wolves and bears."

"That's not funny," he says.

It's really not. But it's probably true.

"I don't care where I go on my honeymoon."

"OK," he says, as we make the forty-minute drive back to the house. "Then where would you go? If you could choose instead of them."

"Fiji," I say. "Hey, I'm gonna tell you something serious, OK?"

"OK."

"If I don't come back from Alaska, that's where I'll be. Fiji. Because if Dickerson thinks he can take me in a fight, he's out of his fucking mind."

"Oh, shit, Lyssa." Mason laughs. "What am I gonna do with you?"

I have an answer for that, but it's not one he wants to hear. So I keep it quiet.

"So this whole 'fuck it' thing. By that you mean…"

"I give," he says.

"You give?"

"Yeah, like give in, you know? You wore me down."

"So I'm forcing you?"

"No," he says. "You're not. You're just…"

"Just what? A wild thing?"

"I guess the name fits."

"So you like me though, right?"

"Of course. You're pretty easy to like, actually."

"Hmmm. Well, that's news to me. But I'll take it."

"How about we just start with being friends?"

"Friends?" I say, making a face. "With benefits, you mean?"

"No, not really."

"I'm confused. You like me, you're going to let me have my way, you want to be my friend, but you want me to marry someone I hate when this whole thing is over."

"Look, I didn't say it made sense, OK? None of this makes sense. I'm just trying to make you happy."

"You mean make *you* happy?"

"Me too."

"Mostly you."

"Lyssa—"

"No, it's fine," I say. "I get it. You're the new me."

"What?"

"You know, thinking of yourself."

"Jesus. I don't know what to think about you, OK? I just know what I told you. I like you."

I turn in my seat to face him just as he turns the car into the driveway. It's a really long driveway so I have one more shot at this before we switch gears and go back inside my prison. "Well, if you like me, then… let's just go somewhere."

"Where would we go?"

"Let's go see your mom. Fuck this wedding."

"You don't need me to get you out of this wedding." He stops the car in front of the house, puts in in gear, and shuts it off. "You can get yourself out of this wedding. Just tell your stepfather no."

"Just tell him no." I laugh.

"Yeah, you're a fucking grown-ass woman. You can make your own choices. Why do you let everyone make them for you?"

"I guess…" I think about this for a moment, try to put it into words that won't make him think I'm just some random psycho, and decide on, "Because I feel trapped."

"Well, you're not. Sure, it can feel that way sometimes, but you're not. If you want to leave then here," he says, handing me the key fob. "Take it. Take the car and go. I'm not holding you prisoner."

"Just take it and go?"

"I don't understand why this is so hard for you. Is it because your stepfather has been so controlling your whole life you actually don't realize he's not in control?"

I think about that for a second, trying to make all the pieces of my life fit together in some new way that makes sense.

"Or is it because you're afraid?"

"What would I be afraid of?" I ask softly. Because I know what I'm afraid of. But I'd like to know what he thinks I'm afraid of.

"I don't know, Lyssa." He takes my hand, opens my palm, drops the key fob into it, closes it back up, and then smiles at me. "Make a choice. Right now."

And then he gets out of the car, grabs the dress, and the bags from the trunk, and goes inside.

I sit there like that, just staring at the seat where he was, and think.

Should I get in that seat and drive away? Go back to my apartment, pack my things and just leave?

But then I look at the house and wonder what I'd be missing out on if I left and never saw Mason again.

Am I falling in love with this guy?

That's impossible.

But am I?

I get out of the car and go inside the house.

Because I don't know. I really don't know.

Everything is confusing. I don't understand my feelings. Or what I was doing up in my room all week. Or even why I was doing it.

I feel like I'm nobody. I'm a thing. Just a wild thing and nothing more.

But then Mason Macintyre comes along and when he's close to me… when he's on my side I feel like I can handle this. I can win.

If he's with me, maybe I can win?

Lyssa doesn't take her chances and drive off in the Mercedes. She comes inside, unpacks all her bags, oohing and ahhhing at all her purchases, and smiles the whole time as she puts them away in her room as I watch.

She looks happy and I think maybe she is. Maybe our little talk helped her in some way. She seems... normal. Like herself. Even though I have no idea who the real Lyssa is.

Maybe this is her?

"I'm not going to sleep up in that room tonight," she says. "Where have you been sleeping?"

"The last room at the end of the east wing. You wanna sleep in there with me?"

She nods her head. "Yes. I do."

"OK," I say.

Then she goes silent.

"Well, are you tired now? We could watch some TV. That's why I picked that room. It has a TV."

"TV," she says. Like this is some foreign concept for her. "What would we watch?"

"Who cares," I say. "We'll be together. We can channel-surf and make fun of infomercials for all I care."

I wait for her to come back with some not-so-thinly veiled sexual innuendo, but she doesn't.

"You OK?" I ask.

She nods. "Yes. I think I am."

"OK. Grab some night clothes and I'll meet you in there."

My bags are in the hallway just outside her room, so I pick them up and take them with me. I bought some sweat pants to sleep in, and even though I've been sleeping nude this whole time and now Lyssa is gonna be sleeping next to me, I put them on anyway.

Something still bothers me about this girl. Something is off. But I figure, these rich people, ya know? They're all weird. They live in a whole other world than the rest of us. So it's not her fault, not really. She was just brought up in this alternate reality. She really, truly doesn't know any better.

I turn the TV on, pull the covers back, and get in.

I expect her to show up wearing the nightie she bought today. Or one of the bra and panties sets. Or hell, naked. But she shows up in her Disney-princess night shirt.

I frown at her. "What are you wearing?"

"This is what I always wear."

"Yeah, but…"

"But what?"

She told me she sleeps naked. And then all week she's been wearing the Disney princess nightshirts. But I don't want to bring that stuff up. Not the naked part and not the princess part either. So I say, "You bought all that new stuff, Lyssa. Don't you want to wear it?"

"Oh," she says. "Did you want me to wear it?"

Does she really not know how to make a decision? Or hold on. Did she make one? And this is it?

I can't fucking tell.

"No, it's fine," I say. "I was just asking. Come on get in."

She walks over to the bed, slides in next to me, and I cover her up, wrapping my arms around her and pulling her close.

She's stiff for some reason. "God, relax," I say. "I'm not gonna hurt you."

"Sorry." She laughs. "I'm just not used to sleeping with people."

I raise an eyebrow at her.

"You know what I mean. Not sex, just sleeping." Then she frowns. "Unless you want to have sex?"

"Uh… I mean, we've had a lot of it today, so I'm good. But I can go again if you want."

She relaxes a little and leans up to kiss me. "That was not a yes or a no."

"How about you decide?" I say.

"Me. Hmmm. OK. Well. Hmmm." She takes a moment, then says, "No, I'm tired."

"OK," I say, flipping the TV off. "Let's go to sleep then."

We snuggle down deeper into the bed and each other and she sighs. "This is kinda nice."

"Yeah, it is."

"OK. Well. Good night, Mason."

I smile in the dark. I can't help it. She's so… calm and different.

"Good night, Lyssa."

When I wake up in the morning she's not in the bed. "Lyssa?" I call, sitting up in the bed. She's not in the en suite bathroom because the door is open and the light's not on.

So I get up and start walking down the hall. I check her other bedroom, the one where the wedding dress lives in the closet, but she's not in there either.

I go downstairs, make my way into the kitchen and find it empty.

"Lyssa?" I call, walking out in the main foyer.

Then I panic and go over to the front door and pull it open. Because I made a point not to lock her in last night.

But the Mercedes is still in front, parked a little ways behind the van.

I check the garage anyway, because there are more cars to choose from, but the other two are there as well.

"Lyssa!" I call, closing the door to the garage and backtracking through the house.

I go upstairs and start pulling open bedroom doors. But they're all empty.

And then I see the door to the only place I didn't check.

The princess room.

I find her sleeping in the bean bag chair wearing the… teenager clothes. Tight, sporty pink shorts, tight, white tank top, no bra, peaked nipples pushing into the fabric, and the thigh-high tube socks. She has pigtails again. Messy, crooked pigtails like she did her hair in the dark. There is a half-eaten pink sucker on the little table next to the bean bag chair and a pink landline phone next to the sucker.

What the fuck is going on here?

I look around for a cam, because I am one hundred percent sure that's got to be one of her other secrets. She's a cam girl with a teenage fetish specialty. Because that's what this looks like. It looks staged. Like a set. And who the hell uses a landline these days?

She must have clients and they must call her.

I am so convinced of this scenario, I pick up the handset on the phone and dial *69, but there's no dial tone. Fucking thing doesn't even work.

"Lyssa," I say, placing the hand set back. She doesn't answer so I shake her. "Lyssa."

"Hmmm," she says, turning over in the bean bag chair.

"Wake up."

She draws in a long, sleepy breath and rubs her eyes. "What?"

"What are you doing in here?"

She looks around then frowns. "I couldn't sleep last night."

"So you came up here?" I ask her. "And put on these clothes? And did your hair... in the dark? What the hell is going on? Are you a cam girl?"

She blinks at me. "What?" The sleepiness is gone as she squints her eyes. "A cam girl? Why the fuck would you think that?"

"Uh..." I laugh. "Because that's what this looks like." *And also you were arrested for prostitution, pimping, and pandering. That's why.*

But I don't say any of that out loud. Because something is off about her right now.

I'm leaning in her face as all these thoughts run through my head and she pushes me away, then gets to her feet.

"What were you doing on the bean bag?" I ask.

"What the fuck does it look like? I was sleeping."

"Lyssa," I say, grabbing her arm and giving her a shake. "There's a fucking bed right there. You could've just slept in the bed."

"The sheets," she says. Like this explains everything.

"What?"

"The sheets are dirty. From that first night we were here. No one came to change them."

I want to pull my hair out. "You've been sleeping up here in this bean bag the whole time? What the hell is wrong with you? Don't you change your own sheets at home?"

"Sometimes," she says.

"So…" I open my hands in a what-the-fuck gesture.

"I just didn't think of it."

I have a million things to say back to this idiotic answer. Mostly mean things. Things like, *Are you a moron? Are you so spoiled that you're helpless? Incapable of formulating the simplest of solutions?*

I really want to say all that. And I almost do. Because it makes no sense. This girl, right here, in this room— she is not the girl I met in that club a week ago. She is not the girl in the gold dress. She is not the girl who kneed me in the balls and punched me in the face. Who ran, who fought back, who…

Something is wrong with her.

Or no. Because it hits me.

Something is wrong with this *place*.

"Pack a bag," I say. "We're leaving."

CHAPTER EIGHTEEN

Mason is angry with me. That much I know. But I'm having trouble understanding why. I don't know why. So I tick things off on a list.

I left his bed last night and went up to the princess room. I do remember that, but I had a good reason. And I know he's mad that I've been sleeping on the bean bag this whole time, but seriously, I wasn't gonna sleep in that dirty bed. I don't think it's that weird. I also think he has a problem with my clothes. And I don't love them. But they're familiar to me so I don't hate them either.

Cam girl though? That came out of nowhere. Didn't it? I don't know. I feel confused and dizzy. Nothing makes sense anymore. And I kinda felt like things did make sense. Before. That first day I was so sure what was happening. But ever since I went up to the princess room that first night everything went weird again.

Weird again.

What do I mean?

"What the fuck are you carrying?" Mason asks me when I get downstairs.

"What?" I look down at my pink and purple unicorn backpack. "I didn't have any luggage in that room so I grabbed this. What's the big deal?"

"Forget it. Let's go."

He takes my hand and we go outside and get in the Mercedes. He looks over at me as he starts the car and says, "We're going back to the city."

"We are?" I say, brightening at the idea.

"Yeah, this place… I don't really understand what's going on, but this place isn't good for you." He pulls around the van and heads down the driveway.

I look back at the huge country estate and have to agree with him. "I don't like it either."

But I feel weird leaving. I feel jittery and nervous like I'm doing something wrong. My stepfather is gonna be pissed off when he finds out. But he won't be here for a few more days so I try to forget about how we're disobeying orders and just breathe deep and relax into the soft leather of the seat.

It's a long drive into the city. Mason and I are mostly quiet until we are well away from the house and the urban skyline welcomes us in the distance. With each mile we put between ourselves and the mansion I feel better. More myself.

There's a lot of traffic as we start to approach downtown. I don't even know what day it is. Just that it must be a weekday from the look of the rush-hour traffic.

When he gets off at an unfamiliar exit I realize he's not taking me back to my apartment. "Where are we going?" I ask, breaking our long silence.

"My place," he says. "I'm sick of sleeping in unfamiliar beds. I think we both need something a little more normal right now."

"Well, I'm not complaining," I say, leaning back as I exhale out a long breath. "I kinda want to see where you live. Is it a tall building?"

"Yeah," he says. And I think the city relaxes him too. Because he smiles. "It's on the north central side of the park. I'm sure it's not up to your standards, princess. But it's not bad, I promise."

I turn in my seat so I can look at him as he drives. It's overcast and raining out, so the city lights reflected on his face kinda shimmer as we pass under them. Reds, and blues, and yellows.

"How are you feeling?" he asks.

"Fine," I say. "A little hungry."

"We can get takeout."

He looks excited at that. After all my stupid comfort foods, I don't blame him.

And then he talks about our dinner options. Quizzes me on what I like. Fills me in on what he prefers. And then we are pulling into the garage below a very tall building.

He pulls into a parking spot with the number P-9 stenciled on the concrete wall and turns the engine off.

"Penthouse, huh?" I say, motioning to his parking spot number.

"Yeah." He laughs. "But don't get too excited. My version of penthouse and your version of penthouse probably aren't the same thing. I mean, every building has a top floor, right?"

"I'm unreasonably excited about meeting the real Mason Macintyre."

"Hmm," he says, looking at me in the semi-darkness of the garage. "Well, I'm looking forward to meeting the real you as well."

We get out and Mason grabs our bags. He took all his new clothes with him. Stuffed it all into one department-store shopping bag. And he grabs my stupid unicorn backpack too, frowning at it.

"Geez," I say. "Sorry to spoil your mood with my backpack."

"It's just weird, Lyssa."

"It's just the first thing I saw."

"Also weird."

"Whatever. We can throw it in the trash if it makes you so upset." I grab it from his hand and walk over to a dumpster near the entrance to the elevators, but he grabs my other hand and pulls me back to him.

"Forget it. It's fine."

He's right about the building. It's not like the one I live in. There's no cool decorative architectural features to remind you of its early days, or live person in the elevator to push your floor button for you. And the penthouse he lives in is just one of a dozen small, but bigger than most, units on the top floor.

However...

"Holy shit," I say, walking towards the twinkling city sky that dominates the entire length of his small, long apartment. "Now *that* is a penthouse view."

"Yeah," Mason says, putting our bags down near the bedroom door. "It's not your side of the park, that's for sure. But it's not bad."

I turn to him and smile. "I think it's wonderful." Then I look around and decided I think all of it is wonderful. It's not very big. Maybe a thousand square feet. But it's interesting. The kitchen is elevated a few steps up and it's modern and beautiful with dark gray cabinets, black countertops, and stainless-steel appliances. I walk up the stairs and turn to look out the window.

The view is even better. And the ceiling is high and arched. No beams. It's too modern for beams. But it makes the small space feel airy and open.

"What do you do again?" I ask him. Because I don't think he ever told me.

"I'm a bounty hunter," he says.

"Princess bounty hunter." I laugh. "OK, I knew that part. But that's made up. What do you really do?"

"I bring in criminals who jump bail."

"Hmm," I say. "How did my stepfather find you?"

He shakes his head. "You know what? I don't really know. Looked me up online, I guess? Or maybe he has a friend in bail bonds?"

"Weird," I say.

"Yeah, kinda is," he agrees. Then he looks at me with a serious expression. "I've never done this before. I've never kidnapped anyone. I'm not a criminal, Lyssa. I mean, I know guys like that. The ones who hunt down people for other reasons. Lots of guys like that, actually. But I'm not like them. I'm one of the good ones."

For some reason this makes my heart hurt. "I know that," I whisper.

"I didn't want to do this job. I didn't want to hurt you that night. I tried to make the van as comfortable as possible and I barely gave you any of that drug. I just—"

"It's OK," I say, smiling as I walk down the kitchen stairs and make my way over to him.

"It's not OK. I took you against your will and I'm sorry. But—" He hesitates.

"But what?"

"But I'm glad I did it. I'm glad I brought you here too. I don't think you should marry that guy."

"Well," I say, blushing. "I think that's the most romantic thing anyone has ever said to me."

He laughs. "Oh, that's horrible. You have low expectations. I can do much better, I promise. Just stick with me, Wild Thing. I got you."

He's got me.

I don't think anyone has ever expressed that to me before. Not once has anyone ever really had my back or best interest in mind. My mother did her best but she was sick long before she was really sick, if that makes sense. She didn't have the power to really do well when it came to raising me.

I can't really say she had my back though. She did leave my real father and marry the asshole. And she let him boss me. She let him act like my father when we all knew he wasn't. She never stood up to him. Not even when she was planning on divorcing him when she got really, really sick.

So it would be normal for me to think Mason is just another asshole full of shit. And when my stepfather shows up here, and he will, Mason will back away and forget all about how he's *got me*.

But I choose to believe him.

Maybe he didn't set out to save me and maybe he's no Prince Charming.

But he *is* one of the good guys.

I can feel it in my heart.

CHAPTER NINETEEN

Just getting her away from that house makes a difference. I'm sure of it. I could feel her change during the drive. She got more relaxed. She perked up and took an interest in things. She's talking now like she's fine, and not acting like some weird zombie.

It's that room, I decide. Even if her stepfather did have the house decorated for her future children, that's not how she took it. That room morphed her back into a child for some reason.

Everything about it is creepy and unsettling.

And I want to throw that backpack away. I should've let her drop it in the dumpster but I felt like there was more to it. I don't know. I can't explain it. But I've been hunting down bail-jumpers for more than a decade and when I get a gut feeling about something, it's generally right. I've learned to listen to that feeling.

I still feel the lingering residue of that house and I have a sudden urge to take a shower. To take Lyssa into the shower with me and wash her clean.

But I don't want her to know I know that something is off. I don't know why. Maybe it's because I know more about her than I should. I read all of her criminal records. I saw all those mugshots, read the statements from the arresting officers, the transcripts from court, and I know what her stepfather did to get her off.

I totally and completely invaded her privacy. If she wanted me to know all this stuff about her, she'd have told me. I mean, how would I like it if she went through all my personal shit without my permission while she was here?

I don't have deep, dark skeletons in my closets, but that's not the point.

The point is… people who care about each other don't do that shit.

It implies that there's no trust and I really want her to trust me.

So I take her hands and pull her close. She automatically wraps her arms around my middle and that feels amazing. I take her face in both my hands and kiss her mouth. No talking, no pushing, no expectations… just a kiss.

She kisses me back. Her lips soft and pliant. Her tongue exploring mine, but not in an urgent way or a desperate way.

Just a natural way.

"Hey," I say, pulling out of our kiss. "You wanna take a shower with me? Hmm?" I waggle my eyebrows at her, hinting that this is no ordinary shower I'm offering up.

She nods her head and says, "Take me there."

I lead her into my bedroom, looking back over my shoulder so I can watch her come to a conclusion about what my décor says about me.

Everything in this place is kinda dark. Kinda gray, but there's a blue tint to everything at the same time. It's masculine, but sophisticated.

My bed is low and modern. Very different from everything back in that country estate. The side tables are made out of burnished metal, the floors are dark hardwood that match the living room, and the slate-colored rug is modern and plain.

She just looks around as I lead her into the bathroom and flick on the light.

I turn to her, my hands on her hips. My fingers inching their way up under her shirt so I can feel her soft skin.

Her eyes wander around, taking in the dark gray, oversized tiles that line the walls and the ceiling. The floating soapstone countertop with burnished metal double sinks. The shower glass that walls the whole space in all the way up to the ceiling to keep the steam in. And then she finds my eyes in the mirror.

We do that a lot, I realize. For two people who have barely known each other a week, we find ourselves in our reflections more than most.

"I like it," she says.

"I like you," I say. Because I do. And also because I want her to know that.

"I like you too," she says.

I walk over to the shower and flip the hot water on, then turn back to her and say, "I'm going to take off your clothes now," as I begin lifting up the hem of her shirt.

I go slow. Like she's just a frightened animal and not a wild one. Revealing her stomach inch by inch. Then the bottom of her breasts, then her nipples—all hard and peaked. Then finally, she lifts her arms so I can pull it over her head.

I toss it in the trash can. She huffs out a small laugh, looking at her discarded shirt, but doesn't retrieve it or demand that I do.

I pull her elastic-waist shorts down her legs as I kneel before her, my face directly in front of her pussy.

I draw in her sweet scent and things flutter through my mind. Romantic things. Happy things. Sweet things. I picture life with her by my side. Where would we live? Here? Or would we sell this place and go shopping for something else? Something that is more us?

Would she get a job? What kind of job would Lyssa Baylor get? We don't need jobs. Not with all that money in my account, but people need to work.

I would ask what she likes to do, then see if we could turn that into a business. That's how you make work fulfilling.

And I'd take her to Fiji. No escape plan necessary. Maybe, after my mom is cured, we all go there? Would my mom like Lyssa?

Yes. I think she would. I don't care that Lyssa has a record a mile long. That girl in that file drawer isn't this girl. Not my girl. Her life is all fucked up but I cling to that first opinion I had when the job first started.

Lyssa can't help who she is. She didn't choose to be Baylor's daughter. This is just the hand she was dealt. So I'm gonna forget I ever saw that drawer of file folders until she's ready to tell me about it.

And maybe she's never ready? Maybe she wants to put it behind her and move forward.

I'm OK with that too.

Because there's this little part of me that just can't reconcile the two versions of Lyssa presented to me.

Her stepfather says she's this wild thing. This crazy, out-of-control girl who does drugs, and flashes her pussy, and sells her body. And the bodies of others, I reluctantly admit.

I have the proof. So I know he's not lying. And I did see her in action that first night. Out clubbing in that gold dress. Passing that guy money from her purse.

I think about that for a moment. Because whatever she paid for, she didn't get anything in return.

Still, all that stuff really happened.

Before me, that is.

Because the side of Lyssa I see is one of a thoughtful, playful, somewhat innocent young woman who just wants some space to figure out who she is.

The only thing I know for certain is that Lyssa Baylor isn't the girl I found in that file drawer. OK. So she did those things. But drugs make people do weird shit.

I don't know. I need more time to fit all the pieces of this puzzle together. And the time for thinking isn't now. Because I'm jolted back to the present moment when Lyssa places her hands on my shoulders to steady herself, then steps out of her shorts one leg at a time, kicking off the sneakers on her feet.

"I bought you all that underwear," I say, tossing her shorts in the trashcan. "And still, you refuse to wear it."

"I brought it with me," she says. "It's the only thing I brought."

I can't help it. I laugh. "You only brought underwear?"

She nods, smiling. Blushing. "Because it came from you. And none of the other stuff did."

See? This is what I mean. Girls who are arrested for prostitution, pimping, and pandering don't say shit like that. Not seriously. And she's fucking serious, I can just *tell*.

I stand up and slip my hand under her hair. "Come here," I whisper, pulling her towards me.

She presses her naked body against my clothed one and this time our kiss isn't sweet. Our mouths are open before we even touch. Our tongues eager. Her fingers pop the button on my jeans, dragging the zipper down a moment later. And then she pulls me out.

I'm already hard for her.

She pumps me a few times, still kissing me. More desperate now. Breathing heavy to let me know she's getting turned on. And then she begins lifting my shirt up my body with the exact same precision and slowness as I did hers.

I want her hands back on my cock, but I can't have that if she's taking her time. So I rip the shirt over my head and toss it on the ground. I bend down again, making her whimper, and lean in to kiss her stomach as I unlace my boots.

Then I stand up, grab her face with both hands and kiss her as I kick off my boots and her hands eagerly tug my jeans and boxer briefs down my legs.

Two seconds later we're both naked and the steam pours out the open door of the shower, wrapping us up in a cloak of heat.

"Come with me," I say through our kiss. Then back away, eyes locked on hers, as I take her hand and lead her into the shower.

She closes the door as she steps in and I adjust the water temperature so it's hot, but not scalding.

I want to make sure to wash everything off her. That house. That room. Those clothes. Her fear. Everything.

I want her skin to be bright pink from the cleansing. A fresh start.

We walk under the water together and get wet. I spin her around so I can see her face as the water runs down her cheeks. She tilts her head up, eyes closed, and soaks her hair while I grab the shampoo bottle and squirt some into my palm. Then get behind her, pressing my cock up against the small of her back, and wash her hair.

"Wow." She sighs. "That feels incredible. You're going to spoil me even more than I already am."

"No," I say, lathering the ends of her long blonde hair up with frothy, coconut-scented bubbles. "I've realized something since I've gotten to know you."

"What's that?" she says, drawing in a deep breath.

"You haven't been spoiled nearly enough."

"Oh, please." She laughs. "I didn't even think to change my own sheets. It's ridiculous. I don't know why I did that."

I do. But I don't want to say it out loud.

"Don't think it about anymore," I say. "Now rinse."

She turns around into the shower as I grab the liquid soap and squirt it into my hands, then reach around and wash her breasts first.

Hey, I'm a man. What can I say?

She leans back into my chest, the water spilling over both of us, and I back up so she doesn't rinse off all my bubbles.

I want to take my time washing her. Do a very thorough job. I wash her belly next. Then her hips. She stands quietly while I bend down and rub my soapy hands up and down her thighs, teasing her a little as I almost dip between her legs, but don't.

She hisses in a breath of air as I lather up her thighs, then wash each of her feet.

I do her arms and her shoulders next. Then pause with my hands on her throat. Wait for her to swallow and then close my eyes because that's so fucking sexy.

When I'm done I stand in front of her and see if I missed any spots. Bubbles cover pretty much every inch of her body and she's grinning at me with the most adorable smile. I just want to eat her up.

"OK," I finally say. "I think you're clean. Rinse."

She steps forward into the water and washes off all my hard work and the lingering feeling of filth leftover from that house in the same instant. Then turns to face me and rinses her back.

She's smiling. And she looks so different even though nothing has changed. She wasn't really dirty, and yet… she sparkles like a new woman.

"My turn now," she says, reaching for the bottle of soap.

I feel dirty from being in that house too, so I stand still and quiet as she lathers up my chest, keeping eye contact with me the whole time.

Who are you? That's what I want to ask her. *Where is that girl in the gold dress? The one who fights, and kicks, and screams.*

Where are you, Wild Thing?

Where did you go?

CHAPTER TWENTY

He is the most beautiful specimen of a man I've ever laid eyes on. And don't get me started on his eyes.

I remember them that first night we met. Staring at me from across the dance floor. Locking with mine, then the smile and the way he turned away, like he was playing a game with me.

As a stranger Mason Macintyre is all business. He was so intriguing in those first few minutes we met. Kinda out of place, but not really. Mason is one of those guys who can fit in anywhere. Someone totally at ease with himself. He knows who he is, he's never had an identity crisis. He is confident, and commanding, and in control.

It was a trap that night. I know that. But I see it differently now. He liked me. That me. I could tell. He liked my dress, and the way I danced, and the fight.

He liked my fight.

He liked the chase too.

But what does he think of me now that he's caught me?

Has his opinion changed? Am I weaker now? More fragile? Something to be pitied? Or does he enjoy being the alpha male? In control of everything.

Because I like the way he does that. I like the way he takes control.

"You did a good job," I say.

"You're doing a good job too," he says.

And I know he means the soap. That's what he thought I meant too. The way he cleaned me. The way I'm cleaning him.

But that's not what I mean.

"No," I say. "You did a good job taming me. Because I don't feel like that girl anymore."

"Which girl?" he asks, narrowing his eyes a little.

"The wild one," I say.

"Lyssa," he says, placing a hand on my cheek. "No. I like the wild one too."

"Oh." I laugh. "Well, too late now. I'm all tamed up for you, Mr. Macintyre."

"No, you're not," he says, his expression becoming serious. "No. You're still her. I see it inside you."

"Wild me?" I laugh. "Spoiled-rotten, wild me."

"That's not who you really are. And that's not who you were that night. Don't you see? That night in the club, Lyssa. You were magnificent. Like a lioness in charge of hunting food for the entire pack."

"Hmmm." I chuckle. "Maybe."

"There's no maybe about it. I want her. Not that little girl you morphed back into back at the estate. That's why I brought you here. So you can be yourself."

I just stare at him for a second. Confused. But something about that makes sense too. I was myself in that club. That *was* the real me. And everything since then has been some other version of me. Some older version. Some weak, confused version.

He steps under the water and rinses off, then reaches for a bottle of conditioner and begins to slowly, methodically caress it into my hair. He makes sure every end gets attention. He massages my scalp so seductively, I close my eyes and lean back into his chest.

I don't remember ever feeling so relaxed.

Then, too soon, he says, "Rinse. Then we'll get out and order some food."

"Already?" I ask.

He laughs. "Don't worry, I have more plans for you later."

I rinse my hair, dreaming about later, as he steps out of the shower and starts toweling off. When I'm done I turn off the water and open the door to his arms open wide with a large towel.

When I step out onto the bath rug he starts drying me off. Dragging the thick cotton down my shoulders and arms. My breasts and stomach. Then he kneels and dries my legs and feet, one at a time.

He stands back up and grabs a large-tooth comb from a drawer and starts to detangle my hair. I watch him in the mirror, looking into his eyes. "I can do it," I say, reaching for the comb.

But he pushes my hand aside and says, "I know you can. But I want to do it. So just let me."

He is gentle with my hair. Making sure not to tug too hard. It feels just as good as when he was taking care of it in the shower. And when he's done I want him to start all over again.

"Now," he says. "About clothes."

He walks out into the bedroom naked. His cock semi-hard and swinging between his legs. His large, tight balls visible from behind as he opens his closet.

How do I keep him? How can I keep this man forever? How do I fix my mess of a life and make this my future? I don't know. I have no idea. It seems impossible.

"T-shirt? Or button-down?" Mason says, holding up two hangers.

But it isn't impossible. It can't be. I cannot go back to that old life. I cannot marry stupid Dickerson. I don't even know the guy. And why the hell should I have to, anyway? Just because my stepfather says so? That's the dumbest thing ever. Why did I even go along with it? Why didn't I just take my chances and be true to myself instead of letting my stepfather control me?

Before Mason kidnapped me I was doing OK. And yeah, I was still living off other people, but I could get by on my own if I wanted. If I really tried. And I was planning on that. And then… and then I was in that house and in that room and…

"Lyssa," Mason says, snapping my thoughts back to him. "Which one?"

I make a decision as I look at my choices. But then it hits me that I already made this decision. I just… forgot.

"Neither," I say, walking towards him.

No. *Stalking* towards him. Like a lioness on the hunt because she has to feed her pack. Like a wild thing.

I take both hangers and throw them on the floor. My hands sliding up the sides of his stomach, relishing the tight muscles as my fingertips explore his chest.

He backs up against the wall as I drop to my knees and take his cock in both hands. Fisting and pumping him as I gaze up into his eyes.

Not the eyes in the mirror, but the real ones.

"Don't tell me to stop," I say. "Because I'm not going to listen. Just accept this for what it is, Mason."

He breathes through that statement for a few seconds. Thinking. Then he says, "There you are. I was wondering if you'd be back."

I smile as I take his cock in my mouth. Wrapping my lips around his thick, swollen head, then pulling back so I can give him a tender kiss.

His fingertips grab my wet hair and twist. Hard enough to pull on my scalp. The exact opposite of the way he so tenderly combed it just a few minutes ago. He pulls my head back away from his cock and I open my mouth. Because I know what he wants to do.

And I want to do it.

Then he thrusts me forward, his aim true, because he slides his cock straight into my waiting mouth and keeps going until it pushes against the back of my throat.

I clamp my lips around his shaft. Doing my best not to bite, but right now, I can't make any promises. He is hard, and thick, and fills me up. So when he pulls back on my head again, my teeth do—maybe a little on purpose—drag against the sensitive skin of his cock.

He hisses, then thrust me back in, not caring that I'm not being careful. Urging me, in fact, to let go and be less careful.

I let him fuck my face. I let him gag me. I let him pool saliva in my mouth and choke me with his cock.

And when he comes, he does it in my throat. He is not careful either and that's how I know he trusts me.

I don't want to be babied. I don't want to be some mindless thing that can't make her own choices.

I want to be his strong lioness.

I swallow all of his come. Every bit. And the drips and drops I miss he swipes away with the tip of his finger and offers to me.

I take that too.

And when I'm done he whispers, "OK."

And I whisper back, "OK."

And then he picks me up and throws me on his bed.

CHAPTER TWENTY-ONE

"Do you need a spanking?" I ask, placing my hands on the bed and crawling up her body.

She smiles and squeals. "What did I do now?" she coos, lifting up her knees to block me, but I just use that as an opportunity to part her legs and scoot my body in between them.

"Threw my shirts on the ground." I tsk my tongue at her. "Naughty," I say. "You're very naughty, Lyssa. Maybe you need to learn some manners? Hmm?"

I lean forward and take her mouth and she smiles into our kiss. "Maybe," she agrees.

"You like it, don't you?"

"Hmmm," she says, still kissing me. "I've never thought about it before. Or done it, really."

"Which part?" I ask.

"The spanking. That kind of stuff. I've never really done anything like that."

I pull back and gaze down into her eyes. "Seriously?"

"You're my first," she says, teasing me by squishing her tits together.

"Well," I say, kissing her again. "If I had known that I'd have been more careful with you."

She threads her fingers into my hair and says, "You were careful."

I kiss her hungrily at that remark, leaning my hips into her parted legs and rubbing my cock against her pussy as I slowly drop the weight of my chest onto her breasts. She rubs the inside of her thighs along the outside of mine, reaching down to grab my cock.

"I can't get enough of you, Lyssa."

"Good," she whispers back.

"I don't want you to go back to that house. I don't want you to marry some asshole you hate. But I have a feeling your stepfather will put up a fight."

"He will," she agrees.

"Why do you let him control you that way? It can't be money. You could get any rich guy in the world to pay your way through life if that's all you wanted."

"Stop talking," she says. Teasingly, but not really.

"Tell me," I say. "Tell me what's really going on."

"I don't know what—"

"Yes, you do. You know what I mean. Why were you acting so weird back at the estate?"

"Mason," she says.

"Hmm?"

"We're naked. You're on top of me. Practically stabbing my pussy with your hard cock. And you want to have a conversation?"

"Mmmm-hmmm," I agree.

"Let's make a deal," she says.

"I don't make deals," I say.

She laughs. "Yes, you do." She lightly drags her fingernails up and down the side of my stomach and it feels fucking miraculous.

"OK." I give in, mesmerized by the delicious chills she's sending through my body. "One deal."

"I knew you'd see it my way." She giggles.

"Don't push me, Wild Thing."

"OK. The deal is… we don't have to think about this for three whole days. So let's drop it until then and just enjoy each other."

She's doing that amazing fingernail thing and I'm about to lose my mind.

"Three days with no talk about anything but fucking, and food, and feelings."

"Fucking, food, and feelings, huh?" Oh, God, she's gonna kill me dead with her adorable alliteration.

"Yup," she says, aiming my cock at the entrance of her pussy. It's wet, and warm, and wonderful. "I'll start."

I laugh, I can't help it. And she bites her lips as she stares up into my eyes and that's it, man. I'm done. Dead.

I push inside her. Slowly and carefully. Like it's her first time and I want it to be perfect.

She tilts her head back and moans. Which is just an opportunity for me to kiss her neck and bite her earlobe. She bunches up one shoulder, shuddering as she lifts her knees up higher, encouraging me to go deeper inside her.

I want to give her everything she desires, so I ease forward. My knees spreading slightly to give myself more traction.

She gasps and I brush a piece of hair away from her face and say, "You OK?"

"Fine," she says. "Perfect. Keep doing that."

I push inside her even more and she bucks her back, and moans again. But this time it comes with a wince.

"Does it hurt?" I ask.

"Yes. But don't stop. Don't you dare stop."

I wouldn't dream of it.

I pull out a little, then thrust inside her quick and hard.

She gasps, which only encourages me to do it again.

"Mason," she says, gripping my hair.

"Lyssa," I murmur back. Thrusting deep inside her again.

"Keep going, just keep going."

How can I not give her what she wants?

Impossible. I want to give her the world.

But I want this time to be different. I want more from her and I need her to want more from me too. So I slow down. Still going deep. Pushing up inside her so far, she winces with each slow, agonizing thrust. My forward momentum pushing her up to the headboard until her head is bumping against it.

She grips my shoulders, digging her nails in. I become crazy with lust. Arching my back as I look straight down on her face. My head pressing against the headboard too. My legs spread out on the bed, my arms holding myself up over her breasts, which jiggle and bounce each time I thrust forward.

"Lyssa," I say.

She just pulls my head down, forcing us into a kiss. Our lips desperate and eager. Our tongues trying to connect.

My arms are straining to keep myself up when all I want to do is sink down on top of her and hold her tight.

Her legs squeeze me tight, making her pussy contract and relax around my cock, and I know she's close.

And hell, I can't do it anymore. Even these few inches that separate us are too many. I lower myself on top of her, wrapping my arms all the way around hers. Holding her captive as I begin to thrust my hips faster, and faster until I've got her hips lifted off the mattress and my balls are smacking against her ass with a slapping sound that fills the room and drives me wild.

She comes.

Moans spilling past her lips and into my mouth as she clamps down on me and then I come, realizing I should've pulled out, but unable to care for more than a split second. Because euphoria overtakes me as my come spills deep inside her.

She's still gripping me with her legs and they begin to quiver and shake.

"Relax," I say, breathing hard as one hand finds her knee to push it down. "Just relax now."

She crumples beneath me. Just goes slack and loose. Her head turning into the pillow as I slide off to the side and tug her up close to my chest.

We breathe hard for a few minutes. Our hearts racing until they begin to slow, and then eventually her breaths and heartbeats match mine.

She sighs, reaches for my hands tucked underneath her breasts, and holds them tight.

"Don't let go of me," she says drowsily.

"I won't," I promise. "And I'll take your deal."

"Hmmmm," she murmurs. And I can feel her smile. It's like her whole body smiles. "Good. Then let's sleep for a little bit."

We do sleep. Several hours at least. Because when we wake up it's very late and we're both very hungry. We order take-out at an all-night Chinese delivery place, and eat out of cartons with chopsticks on the couch while we pretend to watch TV.

She's wearing my t-shirt and no underwear, even though that's all she brought. And every now and then she will position her legs and flash me with her pussy.

I don't even think she's doing it on purpose. She's just… being Lyssa. The real Lyssa. Laughing, and confident. Pretty and grown-up. Nothing child-like about her now.

Nice to finally meet you, Lyssa. Wasn't sure if you were ever gonna show up.

We don't go back to bed until almost dawn and don't wake again until well into the afternoon.

And lying here now, with her in bed next to me, listening as she talks about walking over to her apartment to pick up some clothes, I feel… lucky. Very lucky to have seen the real her.

The girl in the gold dress. The one who runs the world. The fearless, kicking, punching, fighting and foul-mouthed wild thing.

I think I love her.

"So what do you think?" she asks.

Well, maybe I wasn't listening. "About what?"

"You wanna walk with me?"

"To your apartment?"

"Yup. We're playing 'you show me yours and I'll show you mine.'"

That makes me kinda happy. Both parts. That she saw my place. Met the real me. And now I get to see hers. Meet even more of the real Lyssa.

"For sure," I say. "We can walk through the park and hold hands."

She giggles a little. Turning to face me and kiss me on the nose. "I like you, Mason."

Oh, man. My heart is thumping and aching in the same moment when those words come out of her mouth.

It feels like the only thing I've ever wanted was her.

"You wanna come to Sweden with me?" I ask.

"What?"

"Sweden," I say, reaching for her face so I can place a hand on her cheek. "To meet my mom."

I don't say, *Before she dies.* But that's what I mean. This treatment is good. Great, really. But she's been fighting for her life for a few years now and even though I still have hope, I don't want my mom to leave this world without meeting Lyssa.

"I'd love to," Lyssa says. "Yes. Definitely. For sure. When can we leave?"

I smile and kinda huff out a laugh. "Whenever you want."

"Today?"

"Today?" I chuckle.

"We could, couldn't we? I mean, what's stopping us? I'll get my passport and pack while we're at my place."

I know why she wants to leave today. Get as far away from her stepfather and this stupid wedding that is most definitely not happening now.

"Sure," I say. "We should leave today."

"Good!" She brightens. "I can't wait. I haven't been to Sweden in a long time."

"I've only been there once and that was to drop my mom off for her preliminary tests about a month ago. I just got back the day before I met you, in fact."

She frowns. "Why did you come back?"

"Well, for you."

"Me?"

"Your stepfather called me while I was over there and offered me this job. It felt like… I dunno. Perfect timing or maybe… fate. I guess. Because I really needed the money."

She scrunches up her eyebrows.

"What's that look for?"

"He took advantage of you. He knew. I don't know how, but he did."

"Probably," I say. "And I don't know how either, but I don't care. It all worked out because I met you."

"Same," she says.

We have three days. That's it. In three days my stepfather will go back to the estate and take charge of things again. Then there will be caterers, and event planners, and a tent will go up on the back lawn, and there will be decorators, and florists, and cake makers, and all that other shit that goes with a wedding.

And a husband.

In less than a week Dickerson Worthington will be dressed in a tux, standing at the altar, expecting me to walk down it and say "I do" in front of everyone.

That can't happen.

And I know Mason thinks I'm this tough girl. This fighter who wins all the battles.

But it's not true. Not when it comes to my stepfather.

He will get his way. That's what he does. What he's always done.

It's hard to imagine why I would give in to him. Even for me. And when I'm away, it's fine. I'm fine. I have confidence, and I feel in control, and I am that wild girl Mason sees in me.

But when my stepfather is there… I don't know what happens to me. I just can't say no to him. I turn into my little girl self. And she is not a fighter. She is afraid. She wants to hide under her princess bed. She wants to run away, and tried to, many times, but she gets caught. She always gets caught and brought back. And it's always a villain who catches me, never a prince.

Until now.

Mason Macintyre is a prince. And I want to ride off into the sunsets of Sweden with him *today*.

Before my stepfather figures out I'm gone. Before I'm captured by another villain and my prince gets away.

I start checking flights on Mason's phone while he tries to come up with something for me to wear.

"Sweats?" he asks. "You can't wear my jeans. They're too baggy. I tell you what, if you wear sweats, I'll wear sweats too. We'll pretend we're working out."

For a second I picture myself walking through the park in sweats and have an instant revulsion at the thought. But then I picture both of us walking through the park looking like fitness partners. Holding hands like a cool, beautiful athletic couple.

And I love it. So I say, "Sure. I'll wear the sweats."

They are too big as well. But Mason just rolls the waist over a couple times and I tie a knot in his over-sized t-shirt. We look at ourselves in the mirror when we're dressed.

I approve.

"Come on," I say, grabbing his hand and pulling him towards the door. "I'm anxious to get these plans made."

"We can't make a flight today," he says, grabbing his keys and his phone as I tug him out into the hallway. "But there's one on Tuesday."

"Tuesday?" After checking for flights I have since learned that today is Sunday. I kinda lost track of time out at the estate. "No, there's one tonight."

"We can't just book an international trip for tonight, Lyssa. We won't even make it to the airport in time to check in. Tuesday is fine."

No. Tuesday isn't. Tuesday is way too close to Wednesday when my stepfather will come back out to the estate and figure out none of his big plans panned out.

He will realize I've skipped out. And he'll know Mason helped me. "We could charter a jet," I say as we get into the elevator.

He looks at me like I'm insane.

"I have credit cards."

"I have money," he says. "Even without your stepfather's payment. But it's excessive. We can wait—"

"We can't wait," I say, a little bit excited and loud.

He shoots me another weird look. Not like I'm insane, but like there's something wrong with me.

"Sorry," I say. "It's just… I don't want to confront my stepfather. I can't see him, Mason. He will talk me out of this."

"Just be strong," he says, squeezing my hand.

But I shake my head. "No, you don't understand how persuasive he can be. He'll just come between us and take control and then I really will be stuck marrying stupid Dickerson."

"No, you won't," he says. "I'll be there with you. I'm not letting you out of my sight for one minute. So if he finds you, he finds me too."

I'm not convinced but Mason turns and takes both my hands, gives them a good, hard squeeze and says, "I promise. I won't let him take control of you again. I'm in charge now."

I let out a long breath.

"Promise," he repeats.

"OK," I say. "Tuesday. But no later than Tuesday. Even if the flight is full."

"If the flight is full, Wild Thing, I will get you your private jet."

I repeat his words over and over again as we walk through the park holding hands.

I'll be there with you.

I'm in charge now.

And I believe him. I really do. I put my stepfather's reaction three days from now out of my mind and enjoy the walk through the park.

We are a couple.

"Well, this is me," I say as we leave the park and cross the street. Both of us look up at my building. It's much taller than Mason's and there is only one penthouse and it's mine.

"Pretty nice," he says.

"It is nice," I say. "And it's the only thing I have in my own name. Aside from that disgusting house in the country. This was the only thing he couldn't steal from me because it was secured in a separate trust that came from some secret account my mother had with my real father."

"Your real father," Mason says. Like he's never considered that there was another man in my life once upon a time. "What happened to him?"

"It's a weird, sad story," I say.

Mason looks at me like he has never been more interested in what I have to say, ever. "Tell me," he says, squeezing my hand.

"I don't know if I can. It's… not normal."

"Not normal how?" He asks.

"I don't really know. He just left one day when I was little and never came back. Then this apartment turned up out of nowhere after my mom died and I graduated from college."

It's not entirely true. I know what happened to my real father. My stepfather told me that story often enough when I was small. Trying to make a point I guess. That he left. He chose to leave me and my mother behind. And that my stepfather was in control of my life now, the same way he was in control of my mother's.

But it's not a story you tell people. Not even a guy like Mason.

"You never tried to contact him? And he never tried to contact you?"

But I can see he's not going to let this go. So I have to tell him some of it.

"No," I say. "He didn't come to my mother's funeral. He's not even on my birth certificate anymore because it was changed after the adoption. And that happened back when I was seven, and by that time… I don't know how to explain it. I was just… Lyssa Baylor. I don't even remember my first last name. And no one will tell me now."

That part is true. I really don't know who he is. I can't even remember his face. My stepfather got rid of all my mother's photos of him.

"Hmmm," Mason says. "But he must be somebody important if he and your mother put together such an extravagant gift as this?"

"You'd think," I say. "But… I doubt it."

I spot the doorman as we approach and smile, ready to say hi, but he's busy with another tenant and doesn't see me. Inside everyone is busy so even though I'm polite to everyone here and normally say hello, I don't get a chance.

Mason follows my lead, still holding my hand, as we walk to the elevator. Inside, when the doors open, I scowl at the elevator attendant. "Who are you?"

"Charles, ma'am. And you are?" He gives me a tight smile. "I'm new here."

"Lyssa Baylor."

"Ah, top floor it is," he says, entering a key card and pushing the button for my apartment.

I glance at Mason and sigh. He raises his eyebrows at me and smiles. *Be patient,* that smile says. *New guy.*

Fine.

But I know these building people. They are like friends and I had to walk in like a nobody. It kinda kills my good mood.

The elevator doesn't open up into my apartment, thank God. That's always freaked me out. So we get off in the hallway outside the double doors of my apartment and I punch in the security code to unlock it.

The lock beeps green and Mason opens the door wide and waves me forward in front of him like a gentleman.

A loud noise fills my ears and then everything happens in slow motion.

Mason's body jerks back and falls to the floor.

I scream, and someone grabs me, putting a hand around my mouth. I kick, and fight, and elbow them in the ribs.

But there's another man and then another and another. And three large blocks of pure muscle wrestle me to the ground and stick something sharp into my upper arm. It burns.

I bite the hand covering my mouth, still kicking, and writhing, then scream when he pulls it off my face.

But they flip me over, face down, and I have to turn my head so I don't smash my nose into the cold, stone floor.

My stepfather stands off to the side, hands behind his back, rocking on his heels like this is just another day. Just another fight with Lyssa. Just one of many.

"Be a good girl now, Lyssie. It's OK. I'm going to take you home now."

I breathe hard, screaming curses at him. "You asshole! You fucking asshole! What did you do?"

One man places a knee on my back, forcing all the air out of my lungs, and I feel like I'm going to suffocate. They hold me like that for several minutes as I writhe and fight.

"You will marry Dickerson Worthington, Lyssie. It's all set up. And you will live in that house as his wife. You will be the woman I've spent all these years turning you in to."

"You're sick," I say. "You're so sick."

"No, sweetie. It's you who's sick. But don't worry, we're going to take care of you. We're going to make sure everyone knows how sick you are and get you the help you need."

I look at Mason, collapsed on the floor next to me. "What did you do?" I scream. But it's weak. I can barely breathe.

"He overstepped and filled your head with delusions." My stepfather *tsks* his tongue. "It's a good thing I had people watching the house. Just forget about him now. I'll take care of everything and no one will know what happened here but us."

His men pull me to my feet but I'm already wobbly from the drug. They have to hold me up and my feet drag across the floor as we leave the apartment.

The elevator door is open and waiting, the unfamiliar operator pressing the buttons for the lowest garage level where deliveries come in.

And then I just… fade away.

I come to a few times before I really have enough sense to realize I'm awake. It takes a few more times before I remember what happened and another thirty seconds to open my eyes and realize I'm… at home. In bed.

I turn over, trying to see my clock, and then groan loudly. "*Fuuuuuck.*" Because my head is pounding.

No clue what happens to time after that. It just fades because the next time I wake up it's dark and it wasn't the last time I opened my eyes.

"Lyssa," I whisper.

I reach for her. Hopeful that I was just dreaming. That we never woke up, never walked through the park or went up to her apartment.

But the bed is empty except for me.

"Lyssa," I moan. "What the fuck happened?"

Her stepfather. I remember now. Her stepfather was waiting when we walked in. I guess that asshole really does have a team of mercenaries. Because they shot me with something.

I pat my chest with my eyes closed, checking for a wound. Then remember I was hit in the neck.

"Ahhh," I groan. Yeah. That hurts when I touch it. A swollen lump has risen up from the muscle.

When I finally have enough coordination and sense to sit up and swing my feet over the side of the mattress, I have to hold my head in my hands to handle the throbbing.

I glance at the clock. It says five AM.

But the date is what stops me cold. Three days. I've been out for three days.

That motherfucker could've killed me.

My stomach is rumbling. My mouth is dry. I could've died of dehydration.

And he took Lyssa.

Oh, I am just pissed off now.

When I can walk I go straight for the bathroom and gulp water from the sink. Then turn on the shower and sit in it until I almost feel normal.

The next time I look at the clock I'm pulling on clothes and it says it's past six now.

I need to get out to that estate. I can still get her before the wedding. Still save her like I promised.

What must she think of me right now?

My cell rings and I realize it's on the kitchen counter.

'Blocked Call' lights up on the screen.

But I don't need to see a name to know who's calling. I tab accept and say, "What?"

"I'm very happy you're awake, Mr. Macintyre."

"You motherfucker," I say. "Where's Lyssa?"

"She's at home. Where she belongs."

"You can't just drug people and then take them against their will."

"No," he says. "I suppose that would be a very bad idea. Probably be considered kidnapping. Probably spend a lot of time in prison for that. You would know, right? You kidnapped her the weekend before last. You're practically a pro at kidnapping."

"You hired me, you piece of shit."

"I did no such thing."

"Lyssa knows—"

"Lyssa knows, yes. She has described her encounters with you in great detail. I never pegged you as a rapist, Macintyre. I should've done a better background check."

Rapist. Kidnapper.

So that's the game he wants to play.

"What the fuck do you want?" I ask.

"Just stay away, Mason. That's it. You got your money. Your mother is getting her treatment. Leave it alone. Your job is done and I'm sorry for drugging you, but Lyssa has a destiny and you are not part of it."

No. I shake my head and lean against the kitchen counter. No. This isn't how it ends.

"You're sick, you know that?" I say.

"I'm just her father, Mason. I love her."

"You love her?" I say.

"Of course. She's my most precious possession in the entire world. And I've spent the last twenty years putting this plan in place."

"What *plan*?"

"Hm," he says. And I can tell he's smiling. Maybe even laughing. "I'm afraid that's my personal business, son. But your job is done, you did it well. She's better.

Thank you for that. She morphed right back into the compliant little girl I need her to be now."

"What?"

"So be a good boy now and just run along. Forget about my daughter. Believe me, she has forgotten about you. She's home now. In her room. Happy and content being... *herself*."

"No," I say. "That's not her. I don't know what you did, but that's not her. I saw the real her that first night I met her. Everything else... that's *you*."

"Hmmm," he says again. I know what that noise means now. Not just smiling or laughter. It's satisfaction. "Bye, Mason. Thank you for breaking her for me."

And the call fails.

What the fuck just happened?

I stumble back into the bedroom and sit on the bed. Feeling sick to my stomach over the part I played in his disgusting plan.

I kidnapped her from her normal life. Her normal self. And I took her back to him. I did everything he wanted me to.

I broke her.

I did that.

On purpose.

For him.

"Oh, fuck." I lean over and prop my head in my hands.

And that's when I see her stupid unicorn backpack. Kinda peeking out from under a towel near the bathroom. I must've tossed the towel on the floor and it landed on the backpack.

I get up, grab it, and sit back down. Open it up and start pulling out sexy underwear. Her sick fuck of a stepfather probably has her dressed in cotton panties and training bras by now. Knee-high tube socks and pigtails.

I reach for the last sexy bra and find… a cell phone?

She had a cell phone? Where did she get a cell phone? Her purse… she left that in the bar. She sure as fuck didn't have it in the van.

It's a very old flip phone. A burner phone, I realize. And there's a list of missed message notifications on her home screen.

Daddy. They are all from Daddy.

I close my eyes and pray I don't see something I can't unsee. Then open them again and press the message to bring up the full stream.

And I lean over and puke right on my floor.

There are pictures of her. She was sending him daily pictures from that princess room. And there are messages to go with them.

Her father's messages start out innocent enough. *How are you doing? Feeling better? I'm so glad you're safe now.*

And Lyssa's responses are wild and angry, as they should be. *Fuck you. I hate you. I hope you rot in hell.*

But as the days go on, they change. Hers, not his.

His are all the same. *I miss you. I'm glad you're safe. I'm so glad you're home where we can take care of you.*

But hers... hers lose all the fight with each passing day.

I don't feel right. I want to go home. Please don't do this.

And his... *Send me a photo, Princess. So I know you're getting better.*

Which she does. Just her pouty face.

At first.

But then her messages morph into, *I won't be bad anymore. I promise. I'll do what you want. I'll be good from now on.*

And his stay the same. *Send me a photo, Princess. So I know you're getting better.*

Then hers become... *I miss you. Will you come see me?*

And the pictures that follow are not just of her face. And she no longer needs his prompting.

She sends them on her own.

I want to throw this phone at the wall. I even raise my arm up to do that when logical me takes over.

No.

I can use this this. I can use this to free her. There has to be something in this phone that will help me do that.

There is a way to fix this, I just need to think clearly and figure it out. Put all the information I gathered about her and from her and come up with the real reason why all this shit is happening.

So I pace in front of my windows and start from the beginning. Putting the pieces together like a puzzle. Like Lyssa is one of my bond jumpers and it's my job to figure out where she is and how to get her in my possession.

First clue. Lyssa in the bar. Gold-dress Lyssa. Wild Thing Lyssa.

That was the real her. Not the one I found in the files in that office, because that's yet some other version of Lyssa I don't understand yet.

That girl who danced and laughed. That girl who fought back and kneed me in the balls. Punched me in the face and did everything she could to get away from me that night. That was the real deal.

She is the Wild Thing. But that's not bad. That's good, actually.

Second clue. Lyssa at the house. She changed into someone else almost immediately after her stepfather showed up.

I helped her. I feel horrible about that. I played right into her stepfather's scheming and helped her change.

The punishments. My doing. The kid clothes and food, his doing. But I delivered them to her. Just like I was supposed to.

And now that I've seen these messages on this phone, some of that makes sense.

But not all of it.

Because there's the third clue. The long criminal record.

I have no doubt that record is real. No doubt at all. It's just everything about those charges... that's fake. I know it. It's got to be fake. That's not my Lyssa. That's not any version of Lyssa I can imagine.

Then the fourth clue. The deed to the house.

This is the part I can't prove and need to. This is the part—if my suspicions are correct—that will make this whole disgusting thing make sense.

And then what?

I think about this for a few seconds. My heart thumping inside my chest.

The last clue came from Lyssa herself when we were walking through the park towards her apartment.

That. That right there is the last piece of this puzzle.

Now… what do I do with it?

I have a friend who writes wedding announcements in the paper for socialites in the city. I haven't seen her in a while but when I call her and tell her what I need to know—did they get married early? Or is this wedding still happening on Saturday?—she's willing to give that information up for nothing.

No. The wedding is on schedule as planned.

Which means I have time.

Her stepfather is pretty damn sure of himself. Pretty damn certain I won't show up last minute and make everything go to hell because I haven't heard a word from him or any of his associates since that last call.

He is untouchable, after all. He said that to my face.

But no one is untouchable.

Not even him.

I just need to find someone just as powerful who might take my side.

Good thing I hunt people for a living.

Maybe I'm not the good guy I made myself out to be when Lyssa and I were together, but there's people out there worse than me, that's for sure.

I see my stepfather. His mouth is moving and I'm pretty sure words are coming out.

But I can't hear him.

This doesn't worry me like it used to. The first time it happened I was around twelve. He'd become insufferable on school breaks. So much so that I begged my mom to send me places for breaks. Sometimes I went to friends' homes, but more often than not, I was sent to a spa or some kind of camp.

But it was Christmas when I first stopped hearing him, so I was home. I told my mother and she took me to a few doctors, who diagnosed high stress levels and told her to make my life easier.

My stepfather blew up when he heard that. Literally lost his mind.

How could she be stressed? Look at this home I provide? Look at that school I pay for? What could she possibly be stressed about?

And I get it. It does seem a little absurd if you only saw me from the outside.

If I only had a way to show people the inside. Maybe then they'd understand?

Not him, of course. He knew exactly what I was stressed about.

My mother was already very sick back then. She was weak, and depressed, and probably bi-polar, though she, nor anyone else, ever told me that.

When you looked at my mother you saw her future and it was blank.

I was actually amazed she made it as long as she did.

But back then she wasn't so bad yet.

She took pills and sometimes I took them too.

But the biggest difference between my mother and me was how my stepfather treated our issues. He wanted her to rest in the dark and not be disturbed. He wanted me to come to work with him.

This is why I stopped coming home on breaks and this was why I decided I didn't want to hear him anymore and just… shut him out.

I didn't understand the transient deafness back then but I didn't care. If I couldn't hear him I didn't have to listen when he put the clothes out and ordered me to get dressed. I didn't have to listen when he told me how to do my hair. I didn't have to listen to any of it.

Of course, by then I already knew what to do.

So I did it.

I'd put the clothes on, and someone would put my hair up in a childish style, and he always made me lick a sucker when we entered his private offices at work.

He didn't touch me. Ever. And neither did his friends.

Not with their hands.

But they did touch me with their eyes. Sometimes reaching inside their pants to massage themselves. And then there would be moaning and a stain would appear between their legs.

All the while I had to lick that sucker.

But it's what they *talked about* when I was with them that really made me stop wanting to hear things.

I didn't want to know.

I wasn't really deaf. I just… stopped being present and went through the motions. Because there was no way out of this. I understood that from the very beginning.

Ever since he came in our lives and offered my parents an *indecent proposal.*

I can't say I remember much from the days before I became Lyssa Baylor. I don't remember my father's face at all. But I do remember how my parents would fight about money. And how I was always hungry and sometimes, I was cold too.

And then one day I was never hungry or cold again.

I know my father sold us. My stepfather told me this over, and over, and over again when I was young.

He didn't love you or your mother, Lyssa. I am the only one who loves you. And do you see what I've given you?

Yes, I saw it. I never did manage to trick my brain into transient blindness.

So these office visits with his friends went on for a few years before he managed to convince my mother that I needed to come home from school so I could be more involved locally.

By then the coping mechanism had mostly worn off. He was too loud not to hear. So I acted out. I tried to be something he didn't want.

It just never worked.

He never stopped wanting me. Even now, after all I've done to convince him that I'm not worth it, he still wants me.

I am still worth it.

Because who else is he going to get to run this estate?

And of course, even though I didn't hear the plans they made for me, I *did* hear the plans they made for me.

I just tucked it away into a little compartment in my brain and left it alone.

Everything started to change in college. Every day I was away from him I got better. Just like back in boarding school. Only now he couldn't make me come home.

But he didn't have to. My mother was very sick by then and if I left her, who would she have at the end?

So it's a nice surprise when I wake up from my second kidnapping in less than two weeks and I realize my father is talking…

But I can't hear him.

I show up at the estate on Saturday in Lyssa's Mercedes and without an invitation. I didn't expect to drive right up to the house. I did my homework and I have first-hand knowledge of what his personal mercenary team can do. So when the security stops me at the end of the driveway, I tell them I'm just returning the car.

I'm sure they've got a picture of me on their little clipboards because the one in charge walks off to the side to call up to the house.

He stares at me under the shade of a tree, nodding his head. I raise my hand and say, "You tell Baylor I'm sending him a text."

And then I send it.

Thirty seconds later I'm being waved into the circular driveway and a valet opens my door for me. I hand him the keys, straighten my smart-casual jacket, and walk up the front steps.

Her stepfather is waiting for me in the middle of the foyer, already excusing himself from his guests and panning his hand at the office doors.

We enter the office and he says, "I didn't expect to see you here, Mason."

"I guess you don't know me as well as you thought."

He closes the door and says, "What do you want?"

"You saw the picture. I found it in the backpack she brought to my apartment. I guess your mercenaries didn't search my place very well. Because leaving that behind for me to find—*huge* mistake."

"How much?" he says.

"What?"

"What will it take to make you go away, Macintyre? Another five million?"

I just blink at this asshole. Because he's real. This fucker is real. "I want Lyssa."

"The wedding is about to start. We don't have time—"

"No, you don't." I cut him off. "You're out of time, Baylor. Get Lyssa down here right now, or I'll—"

"You'll what?"

"You know what. You dressed her up like a fucking doll. Made her act like a teenager and…"

But I can't even fucking say the words out loud. It's too disgusting.

"Fucked her?" Baylor laughs. "No. I never fucked her. And if she told you that—"

"She didn't tell me anything like that," I say. "You got all your dirty secrets locked up real tight, don't you?"

He sighs. Like he's getting bored with me. "You've got it backwards, Mason. She wanted *me*. All these years, she wanted me. She sends me texts of herself. All the time. That whole week you were here with her? She was sexting me from that princess room. Opening her legs, and playing with herself, and—"

"Liar," I snarl.

"I'm afraid not, son." He pulls out his phone, taps the screen a few times, then thrusts it at me.

Photos of Lyssa doing exactly what he said.

Which I already knew about. Because I found her phone.

But that's not the whole story. Not even close.

"Here," he says. "Take it. Look through all of them. This goes back *years*."

I take the phone and check the stream. "Yeah," I say. "Yeah, it does. You've been manipulating her a very long time. Maybe even since the day you met her."

Which just makes me sick.

"I don't know what you're talking about, son. I've done my best to protect my daughter."

"Your *step*daughter," I remind him.

"Whatever," he says, waving his hand in the air. "The point is… she's ill. Clearly you can see that from the texts she's been sending me. She's done other things, Macintyre. Disgusting things you don't even want to know about."

"Oh, I already know," I say. "I found your files over there and read them all. Every fucking word."

"Good," he says, straightening the lapels on his tux. "Good. I'm glad you took the time to familiarize yourself with her. So you know what she's done in the past. And yet… here you are. Why, Mason? Why are you bothering with this one, mentally ill girl?"

How far will he takes this?

All the way, I decide. This shit he's running demands that much.

"Why didn't you get her off?"

"Excuse me?"

"The charges," I say.

"If you read her criminal files the way you claimed, then you know I did *get her off*, as you put it. Every single charge was handled."

"Yeah," I say. "I saw that. Except… it wasn't. Not really."

He squints his eyes at me.

"She was found guilty."

"Because she *was* guilty."

"But then sentencing. Nothing but fines and community service."

"Because I care about her and didn't want her to go to prison."

"Yeah," I say again. "She'd have gone away for a long time if you didn't pay off that judge. And then what would you do?" I ask.

"Again, Mr. Macintyre, I'm lost. What is your point?"

"The house," I say. "What would you do with this estate if Lyssa was in prison? I mean," I have to shake my head and laugh. Because this man… he is like a goddamned pillar of evil. "If she was in prison she'd be outside your control. And if she was outside your control she wouldn't be here as your little figurehead. And then how would you run this place?"

He stares at me for a few moments. He knows I know. I can see it in his eyes.

It's not panic. Not yet. He probably thinks he can make me go away. In his world money makes everything go away.

"I think it's time you leave," he says.

Oh, no. His response is nothing as simple as just asking. He is making *plans* for me right now.

There is a bustle outside the office and I see Lyssa, walking down one of the staircases, dressed in… not the dress I bought her.

The pink one. The one she used to wipe come off her face.

"Lyssa," I say, reaching for the door handle and pulling it open.

But Baylor's firm hand on my arm stops me from rushing forward to grab her hand and take her out of here.

"Lyssa!" I call again.

She looks at me with blank eyes. Defeated eyes. Destined to live out her stepfather's sick fantasy for the rest of her life.

But I say, "No."

"Get back in here," Baylor growls, closing the door again. "She's a sick, sick girl. You knew this when you took the job. And you took advantage of her just as much as I do. I have it all on film. I have cameras everywhere."

"Even up in the princess room?" I ask, raising one eyebrow. "Because I'd like to take a look at that footage. See if it matches what I have."

He points his finger in my face and says, "You're going to walk out of here and never come back, do you hear me? And if you utter one word of these lies to anyone, I will take you down. I will have your mother kicked out of that treatment facility, and I will bury her, and *you*, at the same time. Whatever you think you know, you're wrong. And you're in way over your head, son."

I slap his finger out of my face.

"You saw the texts, you saw the pictures," he says.

"Yeah," I say. "I did. But I saw them first on *her phone*. Not yours."

He just stares at me. Then swallows. Because he fucked up. And now he knows it. Didn't he wonder how she was sending him pictures? Or is this asshole so full of himself he thought he was home free? He thought I was just another greedy motherfucker on his payroll and this was a done deal?

Well, surprise. I'm not.

He finally says, "I don't know what you're talking about."

"Oh, but you do. You do. You've understood every fucking word I just spoke. I don't think that criminal record is real. I think it's even possible you encouraged her to drink and do drugs. Because you needed her to be Wild Thing, didn't you? And then you set her up."

He's shaking his head, but not denying it. I don't think Baylor is used to being called on his shit.

"I know what you're doing with this house," I say. It's not entirely true. I'm guessing. But I'm a good guesser. So I continue without showing any signs of bluffing. "I know about the arranged marriage, and I know all about the photos, *Baylor*. Because you erased messages in your stream just in case anyone ever found out about your little obsession with your daughter. But you didn't erase the pictures. Why?"

"What the hell are you saying?"

"I'll take a stab at it. Two reasons, really. One. You're a really sick, old fuck and wanted to keep them to look at. And two. You need them as evidence in case some enterprising wannabe detective—say *me*, for instance—came at you with the truth."

He says nothing.

"I have them, Baylor. The texts you sent while I was here with her. *Send me a photo, Princess. So I know you're getting better.*"

He almost guffaws. I bet he still thinks he's safe. But he's not.

"What's wrong with being concerned for my daughter? I wanted to make sure you weren't hurting her. I wanted proof that she was OK."

"Oh, wow," I say, running my fingers through my hair. "You are one persistent bullshitter, you know that?" I lean in. Get right in his face. And I say, "Did you ever give her a flip phone, Baylor? Hmm? How long ago was that?"

He just stares at me. A notch of worry finally appearing between his brows.

It was a rhetorical question. Because there were dates on those texts. I already know that phone was ten years old. I found a prepaid credit card in her backpack. The kind you use to re-up your minutes. And that's when most of this finally started to make sense.

"Did she, perhaps, once upon a time, lose one of the burner phones you gave her to message you and your friends? Because if so, that's the one I found. That's the one she was using last week. It took me a while to figure this part out," I say. "She told me that furniture was hers. She opened the desk drawer to show me all her teenage crap. And some time while she was upstairs because I had sent her to her room to be punished, she found that phone and that credit card. And she called her daddy."

"I don't know what you're getting at but—"

"Do you think she did it so I'd figure things out?" I ask. "Or did she do it because she was conditioned to? Did the simple act of placing her back in that room trigger something inside her? Some coping mechanism to get her through her new nightmare?"

"Again, Mr. Macintyre, I'm going to ask you to leave."

"I don't know. I doubt even she knows. Hell, maybe you don't even know. But let's forget about what we don't know, OK? And concentrate on what we do know. You and your friends have a sick fetish for little kids. You used Lyssa to fulfill some disgusting fantasy."

"I never touched her." And still, even though I'm getting dangerously close to the truth, he laughs.

"You don't need to touch a child to ruin a child," I say. "And this place? What's up with this place, Baylor? And if you say it's a gift, I'll punch you in the fucking face. Because it was never meant to be a gift. It was her prison. That's why you made sure she had a very long criminal record. I admit, I was buying it until the pandering and prostitution stuff came up." I shake my head. "You overplayed your hand there, asshole. I know what you plan to do with this house with twenty-one bedrooms. You're gonna fill it with young kids. And invite your friends over for some fun. Close a few deals while you're at it. And you were gonna make Lyssa run it, weren't you? So if anyone ever found out, she'd take the fall."

"You're insane!" he bellows.

"Am I? I don't think so. All those drug charges, *maybe*. Maybe all that really was all her own fuck ups. But you took it too far. Anyone who knows Lyssa would never accept that she sold her body for money. Or sold the bodies of others, for fuck's sake. She went off the rails back when she was fifteen. Why? I don't know yet. One day, when we're far away from here and you've been locked up in prison for a while, maybe then she'll want to talk about what you did to her. But it doesn't matter. You saw a beautiful, wild girl and decided you could use her. Like you use everyone else. That you could buy her, just like you buy everyone else. And then one day she fought back, didn't she? And you couldn't take it. You can't take anyone telling you no. So you decided to take it a million steps further than it needed to go. You decided to ruin her life again. and again, and *again*."

He shakes his head.

"Did you have another one of these estates somewhere?" I ask. "Did it go under and that's why you set Lyssa up as this prostitution mastermind? Or was this just revenge for you?"

He glares at me. "I saved her."

"No, you *killed* her."

"Don't be dramatic. She's right outside this office."

"You killed her soul. And in my eyes, it's the same thing."

Baylor sighs. Still not convinced he's in any danger. Even though I've very calmly spelled it out for him.

"I called her father," I say, deciding it's time to put this sick fuck out of his misery.

"I'm her father," he growls.

"No," I say. "You're not. You blackmailed him to make him leave, didn't you?" He opens his mouth, presumably to lie, because that's all this asshole does. But I stop him. "He was a broken man back then. Penniless. Barely able to feed his family and then you came along and made… what's the name for that?" I stop to think for a moment. "Oh yeah. An indecent proposal. You bought them both, didn't you? He never forgave himself. He told me he tried to make contact a few years after he took the deal and you had him framed for attempted murder and assault. He spent most of his money on lawyers and a retrial and eventually the facts came to light and he was set free. He contacted Lyssa's mother, used the rest of his money to buy that apartment and put it in Lyssa's name when her mother died. He gave her an out and she took it. She was better. She was thriving and then you found me and told me to *break her*."

I'm so angry now, I'm shaking.

"You hired me to bring her back here because you and your friends were done waiting."

He doesn't even bother to deny it. But he's still not convinced he's done yet. There's still a slight glimmer of hope in his eyes that there's a solution to this little snag in his plans.

"What are you trying to say?" he says. "You're calling the police? You're going to get me arrested? For what? Playing sex games with my stepdaughter? It's not even illegal. She's twenty-five years old."

"Yeah, let's just get to the point. I'm walking out of here with Lyssa right now. And you… well, you're going to be looking over your shoulder for the rest of your life. Because her real father had no idea this was happening, but now that he does—"

Baylor laughs. "Now that he does… *what?*" And that last part definitely comes out as a threat.

I was hoping it wouldn't come to this. That maybe, deep down inside, this man had some decency.

But it has, and he doesn't.

So I say, "You know what? Forget about him. Forget about all of that. I sent that whole text stream to a friend of mine—she's actually here, covering the wedding for the paper."

"What?"

"Yeah. So. You know. If you don't let Lyssa leave with me *right the fuck now* my friend is gonna post that shit all over the internet. Forget about the police, and jail, and morals, and the right thing, and how one raises a daughter, and people coming after you another day.

Because Baylor—you're about to have a fucking PR nightmare on your hands in less than thirty minutes."

His chest falls. Like he was holding his breath and he just let it out.

The saddest part of this whole confrontation is that he's worried about his image. That's what changes his mind in this moment. He's worried about what people will *think of him*. How they will talk about him. He's worried about Twitter headlines and talking heads on the news. He's worried about *stock prices*.

Not her.

Not Lyssa.

When I look at her she's still standing at the bottom of the steps. And even though she's all the way across the room I can tell she's crying.

I turn back to Baylor and say, "I'm walking out now. And I'm taking Lyssa with me. And if you ever come near us I will—"

"You'll what?" he growls, mustering up one final act of defiance.

"You know what? Never mind that either. Feel free to come near us. Because then I'll make sure you get what you deserve."

I turn my back to him and open the door. Walk over to Lyssa and take her hand. She said something that first day that comes back to me as I do this.

So that's what I say to her now.

When I come down the stairs in my disgusting wedding dress I hear nothing. My world is blessedly blank. People gather around me, attendants fixing my hair, or my dress, or my makeup. They rush around with mouths opening and closing. Expressions on their tired, stressed faces. Exasperated at my lack of... involvement.

But they too, are all silent.

I can't hear any of it.

"Lyssa!"

But I hear that.

I turn my head to find Mason pulling open the door to the office. But my father quickly slams it closed again. Leans down into Mason's space and begins to talk.

I want to reach out to Mason. Tell him everything. Make him understand. But he's locked up in that office.

Being told what to do, and what will happen next, and that's it.

That's the end.

I turn my head to look out the window and see Dickerson standing in a group of tuxedoed men. Laughing, and joking, and oblivious.

Except, I finally face the fact that none of these people are oblivious. That their silence about what's happening here is just like my silence.

And then the world goes quiet again and I give in to it and start to cry.

But there's no sobbing. There's no sound at all. Just… tears of resignation.

I know we're supposed to save ourselves.

We're told that in many ways when we're little girls. But we're also told, that every once in a while, a prince appears on a white horse and makes all the bad things go away. But… that almost never happens. If she can't muster up the will to save herself, then the princess must be left to rot in her tower.

So I know it's wrong to wish for a prince.

I watch the silent argument going on behind the French doors of the office and internalize that wrongness.

It's wrong. It's wrong. It's wrong.

But... I really need a fucking prince.

The doors of the office burst open and Mason walks out, straightening his jacket. He walks straight towards me, hand extended. He takes mine in his as I stare into those brilliant green eyes, and he says...

I don't know.

Because I can't hear him.

And I think... it's too late. I'm gone and I'm never coming back this time.

There is no Wild Thing in my future.

But Mason either doesn't care or understands. Because he leads me out of that house and walks me right up to the Mercedes. Opens my door, helps me in, buckles my seatbelt, and then...

We drive away.

And still... my world is silent.

He talks and talks and I hear nothing.

We drive for a while. Maybe even a long while. And then he pulls over, reaches into the back seat, and drops a t-shirt and a pair of sweats into my lap.

I just look at them as he pushes me forward and unzips my wedding dress. Drags it down my upper body, then unbuckles my seatbelt and helps me get it past my hips and legs.

He pulls the t-shirt over my head and the only thing I think about is how it smells like him. A smile creeps up my face as he helps me pull on the sweats, then buckles my seatbelt again, and drives off.

I watch his mouth move. Every once in a while he takes his eyes off the road to glance at me. But still… my world is silent.

And I think… *I'm broken now*. It's too late.

But once we're back on the highway he presses the button to make the convertible top fold back and the wind rushes past my face and blows my perfectly coiffed hair. The sun beats down on my body and makes it hot.

And then he reaches for my wedding dress, all bunched up in the middle between us, and hands it to me.

I look at him as he speaks. And even though I can't hear him, I know what he's asking me to do.

I unbuckle my seat belt, turn around in the seat, and throw the wedding dress out behind us.

It flutters for a few seconds and then crashes to the ground, and… I hear birds. And the rush of wind.

And Mason, still talking.

I settle in my seat and turn to him.

Because even though I didn't hear what he said to me back at the mansion, I did hear what he said to me back at the mansion.

He said, "I choose you."

So I stare up into those eyes of his, remembering the first time I saw them. Remember who and what I was that night.

Wild Thing.

And say, "You didn't come in on a white horse. But I guess a Mercedes will do."

My mother... God, I'm almost afraid to say this. But... she's responding to the treatment. Lyssa and I joined her in Sweden a few weeks after I rode in on my white fucking Mercedes and saved the princess.

Or drove *her* Mercedes and became the villain in her stepfather's tragic fairytale.

I'll take it.

We couldn't leave earlier because Baylor stole her passport right out of her apartment that day he was waiting for us. So we had to put in for a replacement.

Lyssa was *livid*. She raged, and ranted, and kicked, and screamed, and cursed, and...

And I loved every fucking minute of that tantrum.

I hope she never stops being wild. I hope it's genetic and tied to the X chromosome so she passes it on to all our future princesses and they will grow up mouthy, and strong-willed, and brave.

"You're brave," I say, tugging her up close to me.

She hums out her agreement and snuggles deeper into the covers.

I tell her this all the time now. Every night before bed. Every morning when she wakes up. Because I said it to her in the car as we were driving away from the estate that day and she told me later that she didn't hear it. And it broke my heart.

So I tell her all the time now.

She told me bits and pieces of what happened with her stepfather over the years. It took her a while because I wasn't ready to hear it all and she wasn't ready to tell it all.

But there's healing in truth.

Maybe there was a way to put Baylor on trial and maybe there wasn't. Maybe it wasn't worth it. Maybe dragging Lyssa into a very public, very humiliating scandal wasn't what justice looked like in *her* case.

So remember when I said I was the good guy but I know lots of other guys like me who… *aren't?*

Yeah. That's how we got justice.

Don't worry about Baylor. His punishment wasn't just the humiliation of defeat.

When Lyssa asked me about my job I told her I was one of the good ones.

And I am.

Even though all my bad-guy friends got a little richer about two months ago when Baylor mysteriously went missing, I'm still one of the good ones.

We decided to stay in Sweden. I want my mom to be near her doctors. She's not cured, or anything. It's just borrowed time. But we all agree it's worth the debt.

Besides, there's a little prince on the way and she wants to meet him.

But there was one mystery left to figure out. Something I couldn't quite piece together. Why was Lyssa giving that guy money in the club?

I already knew it wasn't drugs. If Lyssa was strung out on drugs she'd have been in withdrawal that first week we spent together.

It was kids.

Little kids who would not, under any circumstances, ever end up at a country estate run by sick fucks like Baylor and his friends. She was using all her allowance to save kids from the threat of sex trafficking.

When I walked in to her life she was truly wild. Wild the way she was meant to be. She was getting better and learning how to be herself after many years of manipulation.

And then I broke her.

But that's not the reason I want her with me now.

It's not guilt.

It's just love.

The fairy tale is never perfect. It's dark, and filled with horrors and setbacks. It has a journey built in to it. The princess must live in hell first. And the prince must walk through that hell if he wants to save her. I never knew I was a prince until I met my wild princess. She made me this man I am today.

And as they make this journey, this princess and her prince—first separate, then together—they learn things.

They learn that they are stronger than they thought.

That some things are worth fighting for, to the death.

And that if they do that. If they face the truth together then they get—

"What are you thinking so hard about?" Lyssa asks me, turning over in bed and prying my eyes open with her fingertips.

I smile and kiss her lips as I reach down to caress her swelling belly.

Then say, "A happy ending."

Welcome to the End of Book Shit where Julie gets to blab about anything she wants. If you're new to the EOBS (as we like to call it) then there's two things you need to know about it. One – it's never edited. I write these after the edits and proofs are finished. So you have to forget about all the fucks you give about typos when you read it. Second—I do have a tendency to ramble so sometimes they totally pertain to the book or the process and sometimes they don't. Also, I like to swear and generally just say anything I want. So if you're offended at the end, I don't apologize for that.

When I first starting writing the End of Book Shit back in 2013 I had no idea I'd have to write one for every damn book because people loved them so much. Honestly, it was a one-time thing! But I got so many comments about my unique author's note at the end of the book I just kept doing them. Sometimes I have something very relevant to say and sometimes I just burble on about stuff that makes no sense at all.

This one is mostly burbling.

But I still kinda like it. It's fun to talk directly to the readers and let them know what's up in my brain.

Wild Thing is the last book I'm releasing in this semi-related trilogy (Soon to be called the Naughty Things Series) about "slightly taboo" stuff but ironically it was the first one I wrote of the three. When I start a new book I always put the date at the top of the first page so when I'm done I can see how long it took me. I wrote most of this book back during the first week of February 2019 but it sat around collecting dust while I moved on to Sweet Thing and then Pretty Thing.

I don't think I had quite gotten the hang of writing "less-twisted" and "short" when I wrote it so I just put it aside for later and gave it another try. And it's funny that I ended up releasing them in the opposite order. I wrote Pretty Thing last but I wanted to get that out into the world first. Mostly because it had a direct link back to Five, one of my all-time favorite characters to write.

And if you're counting pages or locations (as us readers are wont to do) you might've noticed that I'm not very good at sticking to the 50K word count either. This one ended up being about 55K. Which is only a good thing in pretty much everyone's opinion.

I just have trouble writing short, I guess.

But… the real reason I moved on to Sweet Thing after I wrote this was because this is the typical weird story that is usually hanging out in my brain. Slightly dark and twisted with a mystery to solve. And I was trying NOT to do that. lol I only went back to it a couple weeks ago and by that time I guess I just accepted the fact that this story was over-the-top strange and I decided to embrace it.

I have done this before. Mr. Perfect and that whole Mister Series started the same way. Mr. Perfect's story starts out mostly normal and then by the end… yeah. We're moving on to Mr. Romanic and his rape-fantasy scenes… lol And by the time we get to Mr. Match Five is there, and Rook & Ronin are there, and fucking Spencer Shrike's son Oliver is the star of the show.

It just happened. I didn't plan it that way. I just can't help it.

Anyway, it is what it is. Welcome to my brain. Where "write what you know" makes no sense because I promise you, I have never been a spoiled-rich brat who needed a hot Mason Macintyre to tame my ass down for a forced marriage and long career in sex trafficking.

If you guys only knew how many stories I started like this one and then put away, never to pick up again, because it was "weird". I wrote at least four of those last summer that are still collecting dust on my laptop. One of them was the first version of In To Her. There were a whole bunch of other dudes in the first version. And a cult. lol (There's something wrong with me). One day I might write that other story. But it's really fuckin' weird, so then again, maybe not. I'm trying to appeal to more readers in 2019, not fewer. Haha

But in between sending Wild Thing to the editor and releasing Pretty Thing I started another book. And I was SO fucking sure this one was not twisted, and not weird, and there was not gonna be any sort of mystery twist at the end… AND, it was gonna be 50K WORDS FOR SURE!

Yeah. Right. lol

I'm 15K words over my limit and I didn't even finish the epilogue yet. So… best laid plans. If there's one thing I've learned from writing all these twisted stories is that those best-laid plans almost always go to shit.

That's coming out at the end of June 2019. So… get ready for a whole new family of hot brothers who fall in love with their soul mates while doing weird stuff.

Most of my regular fans have enjoyed my little side trip into the world of "almost normal stories" and I'd just like to thank you for sticking with me as I move forward in my career.

One other thing I started (unconsciously) doing since the release of The Triangle last fall was this whole idea of not naming the "city" the story takes place in. Johnathan and I did that on purpose in The Triangle because we wanted a city that had everything we needed but we didn't want to pin it down to a real location. So instead of making up a fake big city (because that's a hard swallow in contemporary romance) we just called the city "The City".

You can make up fake small towns in contemporary romance. Writers do it all the time. But a big city is not so easy. It starts to feel less contemporary when you do that. That's the kind of thing I do in my Sci-Fi and Paranormal Romance because those genres have different rules.

So the "City" in these three books is different. I think the "City" in Pretty Thing is probably Denver. The small town they're from is definitely Elizabeth, Colorado. I lived there for ten years so I used that small town to write that story. But at the same time I used the townhouses I lived in when I was a small child and those were located in Mentor, Ohio. (Hey, I told you my brain is fucked up). The "City" in Sweet Thing is more like New York. It has that kind of vibe to it. And the "City" in Wild Thing is wherever. Maybe Chicago. The "city" location in Wild Thing played such a small role in the story it really didn't matter.

There truly is NO CONNECTION between the locations and characters in these three Naughty Things books.

HOWEVER – I reserve the right to change my mind about that. So… you know. There's that. I can't predict when a character or plot from another book or series might pop up in the one I'm writing.

And here's my one rule about doing things like that – If I didn't write it down IN THE STORY it didn't happen. I will often get questions from readers in my Facebook Spoiler Groups asking why such-and-such did this? Or what happened to so-and-so? And I'll usually tell them what I was thinking, or not thinking, when I wrote that part. But I always end it with the same disclaimer. If I didn't write it down in the story I reserve the right to change my mind.

That's because I learned a hard lesson about writing myself into a corner when I wrote my first series. If I don't know where it's going, or even if I do, and have BIG PLANS for these people or this certain event, then I shut my mouth about it until it's necessary. That way I can write a better story about those people or that event in the future if I choose to.

So one day I might connect all three of these standalone books and one day I might not.

And on that note… I think my burbling has come to an end!

Thank you for reading, thank you for reviewing, and I'll see you in the next book – WHICH IS BOOTY HUNTER! The very first KC Cross book that you WILL. LOVE. I'm telling you, even if you don't dig Sci-Fi Romance, this book is hot-as fuck, this book is funny-as-hell, and this book is TWISTED!

Later, bitches.

Julie
AKA JA Huss
April 28, 2019

JA Huss never wanted to be a writer and she still dreams of that elusive career as an astronaut. She originally went to school to become an equine veterinarian but soon figured out they keep horrible hours and decided to go to grad school instead. That Ph.D. wasn't all it was cracked up to be (and she really sucked at the whole scientist thing), so she dropped out and got a M.S. in forensic toxicology just to get the whole thing over with as soon as possible.

After graduation she got a job with the state of Colorado as their one and only hog farm inspector and spent her days wandering the Eastern Plains shooting the shit with farmers.

After a few years of that, she got bored. And since she was a homeschool mom and actually does love science, she decided to write science textbooks and make online classes for other homeschool moms.

She wrote more than two hundred of those workbooks and was the number one publisher at the online homeschool store many times, but eventually she covered every science topic she could think of and ran out of shit to say.

So in 2012 she decided to write fiction instead. That year she released her first three books and started a career that would make her a New York Times bestseller and land her on the USA Today Bestseller's List twenty-one times in the next five years.

In May 2018 MGM Television bought the TV and film rights for five of her books in the Rook & Ronin and Company series' and in March 2019 they offered her and her writing partner, Johnathan McClain, a script deal to write a pilot for a TV show.

Her books have sold millions of copies all over the world, the audio version of her semi-autobiographical book, Eighteen, was nominated for a Voice Arts Award and an Audie Award in 2016 and 2017 respectively, her audiobook, Mr. Perfect, was nominated for a Voice Arts Award in 2017, and her audiobook, Taking Turns, was nominated for an Audie Award in 2018. In 2019 her book, Total Exposure, was nominated for a Romance Writers of America RITA Award.

Johnathan McClain is her first (and only) writing partner and even though they are worlds apart in just about every way imaginable, it works.

She lives on a ranch in Central Colorado with her family.